Searching the

Crocodile Coast

Howard Young

Order this book online at www.trafford.com
or email orders@trafford.com

Most Trafford titles are also available at major online book retailers.

Note for Librarians: A cataloguing record for this book is available from Library
and Archives Canada at www.collectionscanada.ca/amicus/index-e.html

Printed in Victoria, BC, Canada.

ISBN: 978-1-4269-1377-8 (sc)

*Our mission is to efficiently provide the world's finest, most comprehensive
book publishing service, enabling every author to experience success.
To find out how to publish your book, your way, and have it available
worldwide, visit us online at www.trafford.com*

Trafford rev. 8/5/2009

www.trafford.com

North America & international
toll-free: 1 888 232 4444 (USA & Canada)
phone: 250 383 6864 ✦ fax: 812 355 4082

DEDICATION.

This book is dedicated to my ever helpful and loyal friend, Libuse Dessert.

Libuse, here is the rest of the story, as you so clearly demanded, I hope you enjoy it as much as I did when writing the sequel.

Howard Young.
Kununurra. May, 2009.

AUTHORS NOTE.

Readers of "Crocodile Coast Crash" began to harass me as to what had happened to the bushmen and their mates, the crew of the Boeing and, surprisingly, the unlovely American tycoon.

I had terminated the story in the book at the point of the end of the rescue, on editorial advice but against my better judgment, discarding the ending of the story that I had written.

And so, for my own protection, readers, here is what happened.

Howard Young.
Kununurra. West. Australia.
May, 2009.

And the asses of Kish Saul's father were lost. And Kish said to Saul, his son, "Take one of the servants with thee, and arise, go seek the asses."

1 Samuel ch.9 v.3

We seek him here, we seek him there,
We searchers seek him everywhere,
Is he in Heaven, is he in hell?
That damned elusive Quealey Mogul.

With apologies to Baroness Orczy,
The Scarlet Pimpernel.

PREFACE.

IN THE aftermath of the rescue of the passengers and crew by helicopters from the Asian Airlines crashed Boeing 747 on the shore of the Bonaparte Gulf in the North Kimberley of Australia, it was necessary for a search party to be formed to find the passengers who had strayed away from the crash during the intensity of the cyclone.

The rescue crew of the "bushmen" and the two senior members of Norforce that remained on site at Yow Springs after the passengers were all air lifted out were the obvious choice. Their task was to search for, find and rescue those passengers who had left the crash site of the wrecked Boeing, trekking off into the storm after deciding to go and seek out the towns or villages that they were convinced must be close by.

In this view these wanderers were sadly mistaken. All that they achieved was to become thoroughly lost in the wind and rain, in a bush land that they found frighteningly alien. They had no knowledge of what bush food there was all about them; they were, despite the rain, too frightened to drink the ample water available; and as there were no inhabitants for hundreds of kilometers they did not find any villages. They were not alone, however, mosquitoes in their thousands saw to that.

The wanderers consisted of the Japanese passengers except one injured lady, and two who had already been rescued, leaving nine remaining, and the rest of the entourage of the American millionaire, the unlovely Cuthbert Langford Hart-Quealey III. There were five in his party yet to be found, two having already been rescued.

In consultation with the airline, the emergency authorities and the rescue party of bushmen, it was decided that the search party would include Warrant Officer Hugh Wilkins, Sergeant Clinton Strong of the Army Norforce patrol; four of the remaining passengers, footballers Lance Park and Harry Green, with their new found girl friends from the arts touring group Leslie Roberts and Jane Burrows; and two of the airline crew, Second Officer Eric Peng and senior cabin attendant Tracey Leong. The rest of the party was to comprise all the bushmen and their Aboriginal ladies, the "Professor", "Punch", "BBC"(also known as "B.B." for short with affection.), Sam the "Fencer", Bruce, "Rabbit", Harry; with Annie, Chantelle, Natasha and Judy, the Aboriginal ladies. I will reintroduce these fine people, one by one, to you, the reader, as we continue with the story.

The two courting couples, footballers and their girl friends, were allowed to remain because they absolutely refused to be evacuated, being well aware that once they reached Kununurra they would be whisked south to their homes and thus separated. Their time together was precious to them.

Being allowed to remain was, in a way, a part reward for the help freely given by these young people in the passenger rescue, and because Annie and her crew threatened to "jack up", to withhold their labour if their mates were not allowed to stay. A threat not to be lightly regarded.

To the lucky readers of "Crocodile Coast Crash", these admirable people ("Rabbit" being the exception.) will be old friends. If you are one of the unfortunates in this respect, skip right down to your nearest, best bookshop and secure a copy before you read on. You will then be doubly fortunate, having two great stories to read, instead of just this one.

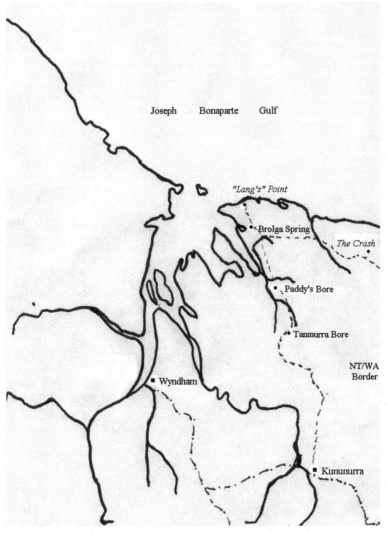

Joseph   Bonaparte   Gulf

"Lang's" Point

Brolga Spring

The Crash

Paddy's Bore

Tanmurra Bore

NT/WA
Border

Wyndham

Kununurra

Located in the Kimberley District of Western Australia.

CHAPTER ONE.
THE CORPORATION MEN.

THE DAY had begun well for the "Professor". Waking early as usual, he untangled himself from the naked Chantelle, found his discarded stubby shorts and began to put them on, under the mosquito net and the sheet. He intended to drive up to the horse yard with the food for Natasha's horses. His efforts to get his shorts on disturbed Chantelle; she opened her eyes, looked briefly at him, and wrapped her arms about his body. Despite this, with much wriggling, he managed to get clothed, and then unwrapped her arms.

She reached down, found the shorts and something else, arising in the dawn. Too late, it was covered, "Later, tonight." he said as he removed the hand. Last night, despite his reluctance, Chantelle had contrived to stage their honeymoon, an event that had surprised and gratified both of them.

Until the last few days, during the crashed aircraft rescue operation, the Professor had slept alone in his swag. Chantelle had been the "sleep in" cook of Sam 'the Fencer', who had ""bushed" her when they arrived at the Boeing wreck, so that he could court Tracey, the senior cabin attendant, who he had met before on a flight to Singapore. The professor was worried about what Sam might do to him, big cranky bugger that he was, when he found out that Chantelle was no longer his.

Not so Chantelle, she wanted revenge for being so easily discarded. Being left with just her own blanket to sleep on and no mosquito net, she had contrived to get under the Professor's mosquito net, then, two

1

nights later, into his swag. The honeymoon of last night seemed to have overtaken them both, the Professor thought, but Chantelle knew better. The Professor managed to wriggle out from under the net, Chantelle was left with just the pillow for comfort.

The Professor and Sam the Fencer were long term Kimberley bushmen who contracted out their skills, experience and equipment. Sam kept to windmill and bore work and fencing contracts, the Professor also did some of this type of work, but preferred the occupation of a plant operator, working graders, bulldozers and similar earth moving machines.

In Sam's view the Professor, with his quiet consideration for others, the fact that he had a wife and a home life and was of a scholastic nature, reading endless books, was not a real bushman. Sam was a man's man, big, strong, noisy, not afraid to get a skin full of beer with the boys in the pub. If you needed a woman, he believed, you grabbed one when she was available, and later turned her loose. Sam was one of the few bushmen who would not publicly acknowledge his co-habitation with an Aboriginal lady, although he frequently had such a "wife" in his camp.

Sam was well built, a big man, not afraid of a fight, but he possessed the asset of a full on frontal stare which he used on anyone who displeased him, most often thus avoiding further physical action. As Punch described it, 'that mongrel could drill holes in a wooden post with that look.'

Sam was inclined to look down on the Professor, but even he had to admit that in times of need the Professor was always there, with a helping and at times guiding hand. They had a somewhat "stand offish" relationship, watching each other carefully.

The other bushmen did not share Sam's view of the Professor. He was accepted by them for what he was, they valued his help and opinion and they worked easily and happily with him. They were sometimes surprised at his "bushman" ability.

Punch was also up, setting the cooking fire, boiling water for the ritual of the morning cup of tea.

Natasha was still asleep on the front seat of his, the Professor's wagon, where she had slept to avoid a confrontation with Rabbit, her unwanted suitor of the past few days. The Professor shook her gently;

"Natasha, wakey wakey!" Her eyes opened, looked at him carefully and solemnly, then that warm smile of hers beamed at him.

"Tasha," he said, "I'm going to take your horse tucker up to the yard, when you've had breakfast, why don't you go up there and feed them?"

"OK, boss, but I'd rather go up with you now." she responded, another smile lit her face as she came out from under the blanket fully dressed.

"Breakfast for me can wait."

He had a cup of tea with Punch while Natasha got her things organised, then, loading the horse food that Gwen had brought for Natasha the previous day, they left for the yard.

Natasha was not a local Aboriginal. Her family lived in Queensland, where they worked on a station that was part of a country wide pastoral empire. Natasha was widely known for her skill with horses and had been persuaded to come to one of the Kimberley stations to train their horses. On a holiday season visit to Kununurra she had chummed up with Chantelle. Natasha had been convent educated and was, to Chantelle's surprise, still a virgin.

This was a serious matter for Natasha; as she was old enough the Kununurra locals assumed that, like them, she was "available." To them, she was "black", therefore sexually active. Natasha was not attracted to any of the men she had so far met in the Kimberley, so was thus not interested. Her resistance to all advances was a source of amusement to Punch and his mates, to them she was just a gin, what was her problem? Someone would "break her in" sooner or later. They would not be unduly concerned if Rabbit forced himself upon her.

The Professor was aware of Natasha's problems and had taken it upon himself to watch over her, partly out of concern for her safety and partly as his thanks to her for doing such a fine lifesaving job with her half wild horses. He was entirely unaware that Natasha had developed a great "crush" on him, something that in her inexperience had surprised and alarmed her.

As they drove, the Professor became aware that Natasha was distressed at the prospect of having to leave 'her horses' behind. He had sympathy for her, but no solution to offer. With glistening eyes Natasha turned to him;

"Boss, I don't want to leave my poor old horses."

"I know, Tasha, they will miss you too." was all he could respond.

"They will be left all alone again, the Station does not want them, they are old pensioners, the crocodiles will get them when they drink at the waterholes."

The Professor did his best to console her, but he could not offer any solution.

The Professor thought back to the marvellous job that Natasha had done for them all, with her little team of three semi-wild station horses, and in particular for the sick survivors, those who were bedridden and could not walk. He and the bushmen had fashioned a litter or stretcher that they suspended between two of the horses, thus being able to safely carry those very sick or injured and who could not walk from the aircraft to the shelter and care available on Attack Island. They were very aware that the success of this operation depended entirely on Natasha's skill and care of the horses. The Professor was determined to see that this was not forgotten.

The horse food was soon delivered; he left a cheered up Natasha feeding her happy friends. It was a beautiful morning. The sun was not yet up, but the sky was clear of cloud, there was a north west breeze, not really cool, but welcome.

As he drove back to the Yow camp the first golden rays of the sun hit the shining, forlorn, bent wreck of the big Boeing; the tops of the paperbarks and Attack Island. The vast marsh, salty gray, extended to the limit of his vision to the north west. The Professor found it good to be alive, he liked this country.

The Boeing was a forlorn sight, sitting sagging in the sand of the marsh, where it had come to rest. Looking at it as he drove back to the spring, the Professor found it hard to believe that so much human drama had occurred at and around the wreck site in the past few days. The safe rescue of so many of the passengers was a source of satisfaction to the bushmen and their helpers.

By the time he got back to the camp Punch had got Annie and some of the girls out of their swags and he was frying some beef, onions and tomatoes. The aroma of good food frying soon had everyone waiting for his or her share, meanwhile drinking hot, sweet tea. It was a happy camp. The Professor wandered over to the cooking fire.

"That's a damned good cooking smell you've got going, Annie and Punch, he observed." Annie's smile in response ensured that his plate would be full.

As he ate, the Professor shared banter with Punch and Annie. They had an easy and long standing relationship. "Punch" was famed as a bull catcher, one who drove a stripped down Toyota four wheel drive to catch wild bulls, those too wild to muster. Wild they were, and big, big meant dollars, too valuable to just shoot and be left to rot. So bullcatchers came into their own; run the bulls down with a Toyota with tyres strapped to the front bull bars, pin them to the ground, hobble their rear legs, leave them to be collected by a four wheel drive truck.

Big bulls, much meat, good money at the meatworks. Punch was good at this work, but he could not work alone, he had to have an audience. So he had a big expensive camp; he ended up with not much of a profit, but as there was "no show without Punch", Punch he became.

Annie chose to be his "mate", living with him until "her skin cracked" and she had to go to town on a bender. Weeks later she would come back to Punch, sick, bruised and damaged, usually bringing a variety of "STD" to share with him. A month or two later she would be mended, fit and well, then off to town again.

Annie was of a short and stocky build, broad of face, she had once been a pretty girl, but her many drunken fights had left too many bruises and scars. Intelligent, capable, a hard worker when she pleased, Annie was welcome as a cook in any camp, and as a camp organiser. In the past Annie had been involved in a short term affair with the Professor, and still regarded herself as "his woman." The Professor , while valuing her as a friend, took care to keep her at a safe distance.

As they ate their breakfast comfortably together, the sun strengthened and more air traffic commenced. A Jet Ranger helicopter landed alongside Gwen's. Two large, self-important looking gentlemen got out. Seeing Hugh Wilkins's uniform, they made for him.

"Are you in charge here?" they asked, without as much as a good morning. Hugh bristled a little. "Who wants to know?" he asked quietly.

"We work for the Harte-Quealey Corporation and we have come to rescue him. This rescue has top priority; you will give us every assistance."

"Bewdy!" said Hugh, as he turned away to get his breakfast. The two important men stood looking blankly at the retreating back.

"Hey, fella, we are talking to you!" one called out. Hugh turned;

"Cool it man," he said, "Have a cup of tea and become human." He turned to Annie, "What are you going to poison me with this morning?" He was rewarded with her wide smile and a very full plate. He moved back to his wagon down the slope.

Gwen had been sipping a cup of tea when the visitors arrived. When Hugh walked away, she grabbed two mugs and took them full of tea to the two corporation men, who were still standing where Hugh had left them, like two bottles of stale beer, totally ignored by everyone else. Gwen wanted her story.

"Good morning," she said, "Can I help you?"

They did not seem too keen on the chipped enamel mugs of tea, but took them so that Gwen would stay and talk.

"Thank you, we are here to rescue Lang Harte-Quealey. Can you tell us where he might be?" A short question and answer session followed and Gwen soon found they had no idea where to look or what to do; they fondly imagined that with a quick search of the area around the Boeing they would find their boss. Gwen was able to explain to them the size of their search problem; the vast empty area took them entirely by surprise, although they were not about to admit to this.

Gwen, reluctantly, took them in hand, and went about arranging that they should take one of the locals as a guide, and follow her helicopter as she began her search.

"I'll see if I can arrange a guide for you. Wait here with your helicopter while I make arrangements." The Corporation men had no alternative and agreed to wait until she was ready. Gwen was well aware of the news value of the name Cuthbert Langford Harte-Quealey III. While he was still 'lost' she had a news focus here, and Hugh Wilkins for company.

Over the few days of the rescue Gwen, bright and enthusiastic reporter for Channel "O" in Sydney, had worked closely with Sergeant Major Hugh Wilkins of the Kununurra Norforce Army unit as he co-ordinated the Boeing rescue operation. A strong mutual attraction had developed between them, to the surprise of both. They were at a time in their lives when they were both contemplating a change of direction or occupation, and their developing relationship thus pleased them both.

Gwen went by Annie's fire, refilled her tea mug, was handed a plate of breakfast, she then went over to the Professor's wagon. He and Chantelle were slowly and with relish working their way through Punch's frying. Chantelle was keeping clear of Annie.

Gwen ate with them, she was in no hurry to find a guide for the Corporation men. As they finished eating, Hugh walked up.

"What are we going to do with these arrogant birds?" he wanted to know. Gwen told them what she had arranged.

"Sounds OK," said Hugh, "Just keep them away from me!"

"Who do we send with them?" Gwen looked at the Professor.

"Not me!" he said, "I want a rest this morning. Sam will go, ask him."

"Where do you reckon we should start?" enquired Hugh.

"I think the best start would be first to follow the track from here to Brolga Springs." The Professor reached for his map, "We know the Japanese got as far as King Gordon Springs, here," he pointed, "That's where two of them were picked up, they were behind the rest of their bunch." The Professor went on, "If you are lucky there might be footprints you can see, otherwise have a look at Brolga Springs, they might have found the old house there. I'll lend you my map."

Gwen went to see Sam, he was reluctant, he did not like what he had seen of the Corporation men.

The bushmen were not enthusiastic this morning to start the search for survivors. This was partly due to their resentment at the actions of the these people who had elected to leave their care and strike out on their own and to a feeling of anti-climax after the successful completion of the full scale rescue.

"Tell you what, Sam, you go first, don't forget if we find them you will be on my film, I'll see if I can get the Professor to go with them next trip." Sam was bribed.

The two helicopters left shortly after. Clinton Strong and his men completed rigging up their local control radio and setting out the carpet for a helipad as more helicopters began to arrive.

CHAPTER TWO.
NATASHA'S ORDEAL.

RABBIT WAS a very shamed and unhappy man. For days he had tried to make it with that uppity little Natasha, to be completely ignored.

"Who does she think she is?" he asked himself, "She's just another gin." A few generous snorts of rum the previous night had given him the courage to sit on her swag, waiting for her to come to bed. He sat there, like a shag on a rock, for almost an hour before he realised that she was not going to claim it. He had been made to look a complete fool, in front of the whole camp. He looked about, searching for her, but it was morning before he found out where she had slept. Drinking tea and watching her, he planned his revenge. When she left with the Professor to feed her horses, he took his chance. He sidled out to the paper barks around the spring, and shielded by the trees he made his way to the fence, and quietly walked up to the yard, hiding behind a tree as the Professor drove past on his way back to the camp. Rabbit was unaware that Punch had seen him leave.

Meanwhile, several more helicopters arrived, a number of men got out, some were from the crash investigation people, and some had come to collect more bodies. After the ritual of a mug of tea, they all flew off to land adjacent to the Boeing wreck.

The Bell 412 from Tindal was one of the machines; the bodies were to be strapped on the skids of the helicopters, not inside. The people at Yow Springs decided to keep well clear of the Boeing for the day. The Professor filled in his time checking oil, water and fuel in his wagon then went to find Punch, who was still in the kitchen area drinking tea and talking to "BBC".

He joined these two, found a mug, made tea and looked around.

The Professor viewed the scene with content. The search party was composed of, for the most part, people he knew well or of those who he knew he could trust.

Out on the sandy marsh, more than a kilometer away, to the west of Attack Island, the bent Boeing lay glistening in the morning sun. Attack Island was only a proper island at the time of rare very high tides. It was usually only surrounded by the bare salty sand of the marsh. In the cyclone storm the island had been accessed by the bushmen in their 4WD vehicles using a very boggy, muddy crossing over the narrow part of the marsh.

There were already several helicopters standing near the wreck, and he knew that the morgue people would be busy loading up the bodies of the dead passengers that the crocodiles had spared, together with the body of the dead Robinson helicopter pilot. This unfortunate man had died when his machine hovered too close to the Boeing in the night of the crash, trying to land to help in the rescue. It had become entangled in the remains of the radio antenna on top of the wreck, flipped aside and destroyed itself on the sand of the marsh.

The Professor spent a short time speculating how many bodies were left and how many the crocodiles may have taken. With a shrug, he abandoned that thought; there was nothing he could do about that.

Retrieving Natasha's abandoned swag from the camp area where she had left it last night, the Professor went back to his Toyota, a fresh mug of tea in hand. He continued with packing up his own swag, rolling it up tight and stacking it on the tray of his vehicle. As he bent to pick up Natasha's swag, he suddenly had a flash of memory from last evening, "Rabbit" sitting on her swag in his fruitless wait for Natasha to go to bed. Natasha preferred to sleep under a blanket on a Toyota seat, rather than go anywhere near Rabbit.

The Professor jerked rapidly erect, looked swiftly about and could not see "Rabbit" anywhere. . "Where is Rabbit?" he called out to Punch.

"He went for a walk up that way." responded Punch, pointing towards the horse paddock.

"Quick, Punch, come with me!" he yelled, leaping into the driving seat of his 4WD. Punch parked his mug, and looking a little bemused, followed quickly, swinging onto the wagon as the Professor spun it around to go up the fence line.

"What's the rush?" he called. "I'm not packed ready yet!" The relationship between Rabbit and Natasha were their affair, as far as Punch was concerned. Perhaps the Professor wanted her for himself?

The Professor was in no mood to argue, he had his Toyota leaping up the track towards the Attack Bore yards, where he had left Natasha feeding her horses, Punch clinging on to the side desperately as the vehicle bounced and swerved.

As the Toyota slammed to a skidding stop at the yards, they could hear that the air was full of female screams of protest and shouts for help, coming from over behind the tin roofed shelter. They ran over and in a corner made by the fence and the shelter found a man lying on top of the small brown figure of Natasha, who was doing the fighting and screaming.

The Professor picked up a long heavy lump of wood from the fireplace and brought it down as hard as he could on the bare white behind that faced them. He had time to get in a second good whack before Rabbit rose up and backed away with his trousers around his ankles, his voice raised in protest. The raised lump of wood over the Professor's head convinced him that his personal safety was better served by running away.

Natasha leaped up, trying to cover herself, saw whom it was, lunged into the Professors arms, and began to cry her heart out.

"He didn't get it into me, he didn't," she sobbed over and over. The Professor carried her over to the cook's seat by the old fireplace and sat down.

"Punch," he called, "Can you follow that bastard down to the camp and make sure he gets on the first helicopter out of here before I personally kill him."

Punch came around from behind the shelter.

"Do you want to do that?" he asked, "he didn't hurt her." He paused, took one look at the Professor's face, turned and left. "Ok, Ok, don't kill me as well, I'll get rid of him."

Natasha cried for a long time, curled up on his lap. From time to time she repeated her protest;

"He didn't get it into me," as if her life depended on this. The Professor soothed her as best he could, regretting that he had not kept a better eye on Rabbit.

In time she quietened down. "What happened, can you tell me now?" he asked.

"I went for a pee behind the shelter," she started to sob again, "I didn't see him, he must have been hiding. As soon as my pants were down, he rushed around the corner and jumped on me." Natasha curled herself tightly for a time in the Professor's lap, sobbing quietly.

Some time later the sobbing stopped

"I'll take you down to the camp now, if you are ready?" the Professor suggested. This was too much for Natasha, she was not ready to face the other women, not sure as to their reaction in what to them was a commonplace event.

. The Professor carried her over to the water trough, she was bruised, scratched and had a very muddy back.

"Natasha, you have too much mud on you, I am going to clean you up, if that is ok?"

"Yes, boss." she whispered, still clinging to his neck.

He placed her down gently, to stand by the trough, took the torn underpants from her thighs to use as a washer, using them to sponge down the scratches, which were not deep, and, her front being clean, washed the mud from her rear and back, using clean water from the trough.

"Am I hurting you?" asked the Professor, afraid his scrubbing might be too rough.

"No, I like the way you look after me, boss."

Natasha, usually so particular of her modesty, surprised him by letting him care for her so intimately. She just stood, watching him with those wide brown eyes, with scarcely a flinch when he wiped her cuts. She was quite beautiful, the Professor thought, a perfect miniature female. Light brown skin, shapely little arms and legs, firm brown belly over a triangle of short hair;

"Stop, keep your mind on the job," he reminded himself, pulling her jeans up gently. Natasha slowly tucked her shirt into her jeans, watching his face, and then climbed again into his arms.

"You will need clean clothes, I can't get all the mud of your back, you should have a bogey as soon as we get back to Yow Springs. Chantelle will look after you." Natasha could only nod her agreement, unsure as she was of Chantelle's reaction; privately she was content with the gentle attentions of the Professor. She was unhappily aware of the fact that the other women could say that she was making too much fuss of what had happened, a commonplace event for them, and to some extent ridicule her. Rape equals seduction in their experience.

"Where is my hat?" she asked. They found it behind the shelter, she would not go there herself to get it, he had to put her down first. Retrieving her hat and putting it on her head, he was surprised to find that Natasha waited to be picked up again. He carried her to his vehicle, intending to put her on the seat, but was taken unawares when she wrapped herself tighter into his arms and kissed him full on the lips. As he returned the kiss, he was surprised to find that she was trembling violently. He placed her gently but very firmly down on the seat.

He then drove them back to the Yow Springs camp slowly, taking his time as Natasha prepared herself to meet the other girls. Punch had told Annie what had happened, under her direction they all flocked around Natasha to care for her. She started to sob and tell them all;

"He didn't get it into me!" The girls took her back behind the bushes, washed her and, putting her into a change of clothes, settled her for the time being in her swag, with a drink and cool cloths to wipe her face.

Punch came over to see the Professor;

"Rabbit is over at the island, waiting to go on one of the helicopters with the bodies. He reckons you are making too much fuss, 'She's only a gin,' he says, 'someone has to break her in.'" The Professor got up rapidly, as if to go over to the island. Punch held him back.

"You tell that bastard that if he is anywhere near Kununurra when I get back I'll come after him to kill him. He won't even be safe in Wyndham." Punch was shocked. He was a rough man, had been in a lot of fights, but the ferocity on the Professor's face frightened him.

"Ok, ok, I'll tell him, you stay here." Punch went on another long walk over to the Boeing and stayed with Rabbit for a time, making sure that he understood the Professor's intentions and advising him where to look for friends and work in towns well away from the East Kimberley. Rabbit's parting words to Punch were;

"What a lot of fuss just over one little gin!" All the same, he made sure to get a bus out of town that night.

CHAPTER THREE.
THE BROLGA SPRINGS RESCUES.

IT HAD been a long night for Sam Wrightson. Tracey had him in her spell, she could twist him around her finger. He knew she was very attracted to him, the right chemistry was there, they kissed, cuddled and petted for hours, but the pants stayed on. Mother Leong had instructed her too well. He was exhausted, worn out with trying, and greatly sexually frustrated. His parts were painful and unused. With the dawn Sam had left his swag, Tracey was still sleeping peacefully despite the helicopter noises when he left with the Harte-Quealey Corporation men.

The two machines flew side by side towards King Gordon Spring, half way between Yow Springs and Brolga Springs. Sam found it interesting to watch the other machine so close. He could see Hugh and Gwen, sitting close and talking animatedly. He was jealous, "I'll bet that bloody Hugh didn't miss out," he grumbled to himself.

They landed near the spring, in the shade of the tall paper barks, and looked carefully at the tracks. There were rain blurred footprints, partly over printed by cattle tracks leading towards Brolga Springs. They took to the air briefly, stopping to look for any footprints at the junction of the tracks from Paddy's Bore and Brolga. Here they found more footprints, some of which went each way.

Sam was amused to discover that the Corporation men were puzzled by his concentration on the muddy footprints.

"Why don't we just fly around until we see them?"

"Ok, you just tell me where you think they might be?" After a consultation, the two did not seem to reach a consensus.

"How much further do we have to fly? We only loaded enough fuel to search around the airliner. Our pilot says we will need more fuel. Do you have any supplies at your camp?" The Corporation men were clearly distressed.

"Fuel, no, we do not have any at Yow Springs. You will have to go back to Kununurra after dropping Sam off at our camp." Hugh could barely hide his amusement.

Thus a bare hour after leaving both helicopters were back at the Yow Springs camp having searched fruitlessly only as far as King Gordon Springs. It was a relieved Sam who was dropped off by the Corporation men before they left.

"Those blokes don't have a clue; they will never find their boss without help. Talk about "Babes in the Wood!" was his empathetic dismissal. "That's a good machine, a good way to travel." was his final observation.

Sam found Tracey up and breakfasted, trying to work out how to roll a swag.

As the use of the local air control system now seemed to be no longer required, Hugh Wilkins gave instructions for it to be dismantled. One radio was to be kept active, until the proposed move to Brolga was commenced. The six Norforce Landrovers were to be packed up, one for the use of himself and Sergeant Clinton Strong on the search, the others to await future return to Kununurra. All the Norforce men were to be relieved and flown out that day. Their vehicles would be retrieved, driven by other drivers flown in when the weather allowed.

"Fit a full radio set up into the Landrover that you keep for us, Clint, so we can still be in full contact. Use an aerial up a tree that we can pull down before we move each time."

Walking up through the Yow camp, with the various paired bushmen couples and their helpers packing up their vehicles, Hugh had a sudden thought.

If he had to share his Landrover with Clinton Strong how could he have any privacy with Gwen? Her gear was in his vehicle, when her helicopter was away at night she camped with him, who wanted the Sergeant around? One less Landrover to be collected later would be a plus, also. He wheeled about and closed rapidly back on Clinton.

"Change of plan, bloke. You get one of the Landrovers ready for yourself, we might just need two. Make sure that it has a full radio set up as well, but only use the one tree antenna for now." Clinton Strong stood a moment, nonplussed, then a slow smile of understanding rewarded the already retreating back of his boss.

Packing up seemed to the Professor to be a very slow task. Everyone was busy, all were doing something, but no one seemed to be ready to leave. When Annie called a 'smoko', they all gathered together in quick time. What did Annie have for them this morning? Sipping his tea and taking a bite of his bread and corned beef, the Professor innocently asked;

"Is anyone packed, ready to leave, yet?" There was no response. Putting down his battered mug, Sam finally spoke.

"This is a good camp, we are happy here. Why don't we wait until the helicopters find something, then we will know where to go?" There was a strong murmur of assent.

"Ok, ok, I got the message. As soon as we hear from the helicopters we will have to move fast. We don't want to be setting up camp in the dark, do we?" The Professor, though not happy with this decision, could see the logic in it. He immediately took Gwen aside.

"Can you get under way now, arrange to meet the Corporation helicopter at Brolga Springs, and search from there?" Gwen understood his concern; she also wanted to get going, finding Lang Harte-Quealey III was her news. She had found the need to conduct the search thoroughly, looking in all the likely places between Yow and Brolga, quite frustrating.

"We'll go right now, listen for the radio in Hugh's Landrover." Within minutes a shower of leaves over the camp marked her departure, taking Hugh and a reluctant Sam as guides.

As they approached the house at Brolga Springs, they caught sight of the Corporation helicopter; it was veering in from the south to join them as they flew low over Brolga.

"Bingo!" yelled Hugh, the first to spot a figure as it ran out of the house. It was followed by two more, a young girl and man. They settled their machines down in the cleared area in front of the buildings, being careful of the trees all around. The Corporate gentlemen rushed over, looking past the three figures.

"Where is Lang?" they asked anxiously, each wishing to be recognised as the rescuer. A very weary, hungry, dishevelled but alert Helen Anderson spoke up, talking very carefully. She paused to look at the cameraman and Gwen, then spoke.

"Where is Lang, you want to know? He could be in hell already, for all I care! The bastard took us with him two days ago to follow that track to what he insisted must be a village. He has no care for anyone else but himself. He bullied all of us into following him into this miserable place, totally ignoring our opinions and protests"

As the camera rolled the shocked Corporate men rushed forward, seizing hold of Helen to try and stop her from talking further. The menace in their approach caused a reaction by a very interested but not very friendly Sam, who grabbed them from behind by their coat collars.

"Don't you dare touch the lady!" he growled in warning, as they turned in protest. They wisely decided to do as the big fellow said.

"What happened?" Gwen slipped into interview mode.

"The big bastard walked in front, expecting us to follow. It was almost as though he was slightly demented. He was convinced that there was a town or village on the coast, he behaved as if he believed that it was being hidden from him. He was shouting and raving, abusing us all for not finding any sign of a settlement. I suppose not getting his own way, as he has all his life, was getting to him."

"One by one we dropped behind, and came back here, where we knew there was water and shelter. Except for poor Steve Roper, he was kept close; we don't know where he is. For years I've worked for that man, the always ready, efficient secretary, thinking he was a clever, busy businessman. He wasn't, he's just a puffed up, noisy bully. I absolutely hate him!" She burst into tears, Gwen moved forward to comfort her. The other two survivors gathered around, supporting Helen by their presence, but being careful not to say much. They were clearly in awe of the two Corporation men.

Hugh went with the pilot back to Gwen's helicopter, to use the radio.

"Clinton, we have found three of the Harte-Quealey mob, I say again, three of the Quealey mob, two women and one young man. They are suffering from exposure, they are hungry, sunburnt and a little dehydrated, otherwise in reasonable shape. Can you have soup and light food ready for them, don't let them overeat. I'll send them to you now. Can you arrange for them to fly out as soon as possible? Our helicopters here are not able to do this at present, having further searching to do."

"While they are waiting perhaps you could arrange for them to have a good scrub up and give them some clean dry clothes if you have any spare. The two ladies are not rapt with the idea of fronting up to the inevitable press conference when they get to Kununurra muddy and ragged as they now are." Hugh continued;

"We have not found the "Big Boss" and one other bloke yet." His message acknowledged, Hugh fronted up to the two Corporate men.

"You will wait here," he said, "While your helicopter takes these three to our camp. They will be fed, cleaned up and sent to Kununurra from there."

"The hell we will!" exclaimed one of the two, "We're going straight on after Lang! Who the hell do you think you are, to tell us what to do?"

"You asked me this morning if I was in charge. Well, now you know." Hugh turned and left, knowing Sam was there. Gwen's camera, they suddenly realised, also had them in focus.

"Might as well settle down in the shade to wait," Sam observed, backing up his statement with a look from his post hole boring eyes. Wait they did.

Gwen was in close conversation with Helen Anderson. The alert, efficient secretary of thirty years was evident; Gwen thought she must be in her early fifties, fit despite her ordeal. She was entrusting her tape to this survivor, to get it to her producer in Kununurra. Helen, aware of the contents, her strong criticism of her tycoon boss and the furore that this would cause, had a strong personal interest in seeing that it did. She had every intention to add to her comments when she got to Kununurra. Gwen knew her tape was safe.

Hugh and Gwen then flew on a further search, but although they followed the track right to its end at the sea, they did not find anyone. They reported this negative result to the Yow Springs base radio as they flew back to Brolga Springs.

Gwen was not surprised to be approached by one of the Corporation men with an offer to 'buy her tape' of the very controversial Helen Anderson interview. It was evident that they wished to both find him and to protect the Harte-Quealey reputation. Gwen's only reaction was a blank look and her back as she turned and walked away.

CHAPTER FOUR.
THE PADDY'S BORE SURVIVORS.

"WE'VE BEEN right to the end of the coast track, no sign of the other two. We'll go now to the Paddy's Bore area, to see if we can find the Japanese. Sam can go with his two mates to have another look out here along the coast when their helicopter gets back."

Hugh was now enjoying his day, particularly with Gwen for close company.

It did not take them long to find some of the survivors. A low searching swoop over the windmill and tank brought seven figures running from the shelter of a small limestone cave in the hills behind the bore. They landed in the cleared area used by campers and amateur fishermen on their way to the coast and back, to the south of the tank.

Soon Gwen's crew was busy again as they landed, filming as Gwen commented. Hugh made some decisions and got onto the radio.

"Clinton, can you ask the skipper of the big Bell, the 412, if he can come and pick up the Japanese we have just found; there are seven of them? Has he started loading bodies yet?" He waited as Clinton contacted the Bell, he could only hear one side of the ensuing conversation. Presently Clinton advised him;

"Hugh, they have loaded only four bodies on the skids, they are well wrapped and packaged. Your Japanese can be lifted and the pilot says he can also take some of our troops, who do you want to send?" Hugh decided to keep back two drivers and Clinton Strong. With the search narrowing down, there was little work for the Norforce men to do. Hugh nominated the four soldiers who were to go. He kept a wry smile to himself as he realised that the Bell skipper was being very helpful, who wanted to load dead bodies when live ones were available?

"Clinton, it would be best if these Japanese are taken directly from here to Kununurra. Let me know when the Bell leaves, we will fly up and guide him in."

Out on the flat, Gwen was having a battle. Language was a problem, made much worse by the near hysteria of all the Japanese survivors. They were still very frightened. The size of the empty landscape that they had wandered around in for the last few days had crushed them.

"Where are the people? Where?" was their constant wail. One of the businessmen, after he was calmed down, had the best English, he eventually told their story.

"We walk, we walk, it rain, it rain, we only see the ground. No dry, no place to sleep, no food, no water."

"No water?" Gwen interjected in surprise. "What about the rain pools?"

"Too dangerous, things living in that water, might be poison. Got too thirsty, had to drink some." He shuddered. "We very frightened."

"Then the rain stop, we follow track, we see where that terrible American go, he frighten us too, we try this way. Here is clean water". He pointed to the tank overflow. "We drink, we wash, and we live in cave. But no food."

"There were eleven of you," prompted Gwen, "What happened to the other four?"

"Two of them too frightened to come, we leave them with big trees, two others walk on down that path, they follow wheels to find a town. They not come back, we frightened for them!"

"Well," said Gwen, "the first two were lucky, they were found two days ago, they should be in Darwin now." The relay of this news caused an excited babble. "A helicopter is coming to take you to the nearest town, Kununurra, in a few minutes. It is ninety kilometres away." This caused chatter, then some shouts of protest. The bridegroom of the little Japanese lady with the injured leg wanted to go back to her at the Boeing. He was totally disbelieving when told she was already in Darwin. He had told her to wait, she would still be at the Boeing, he insisted.

Gwen did not dare tell him that the little lady, far from waiting obediently at the crash, was already back in Japan, having decided in her own quiet way that a bridegroom who could leave her behind on her honeymoon was not much of a prospect for a life-long husband.

The radio came to life,

"Hugh, the Bell is leaving now, will be with you in five."

"Roger, did our blokes get on it?"

"Affirmative, they also took that bloke 'Rabbit'."

Gwen immediately had her Jet Ranger helicopter fly up to guide the big Bell helicopter into Paddy's Bore. As soon as it landed the Japanese were helped inside, the bridegroom putting up more protest. He was bundled in by two of his fellow survivors.

With the departure of the now fully loaded Bell helicopter for Kununurra there were now only two Jet Ranger helicopters working in the search area, that being used by the Quealey Corporation men to try to find their boss, and Gwen's TV reporters unit. The crash investigators had, it seemed, gone home to Kununurra for the day after completing their inspections, leaving the crew looking after the bodies at work awaiting the return of the big Bell machine.

Gwen's Jet Ranger flew back to Brolga Springs to continue the coastal search. In the air they contacted the Corporation helicopter, it having earlier come back from Yow Springs. It had collected Sam with the Corporation men from where they were waiting at Brolga, and they also were searching the tracks to the coast again. Hugh then had another thought. It was obvious that the search for Lang Harte-Quealey III might take some time. Back to the radio.

"Clinton, I think it best if the camp is now relocated up here to Brolga Springs or Paddy's Bore. Do you think that you could suggest this to the Professor, I think that they should make a move now, you can bring the two Landrovers and our drivers with them."

The Professor was more than happy with this suggestion. Within a few minutes he had everyone in action, any remaining swags, tarps, food, pots and pans were slung into vehicles, engines were started and vehicles lined up along the fence line. Clinton offered to drive Sam's vehicle until he was returned. Soldiers, the crew members Eric and Tracey and the four remaining passengers found places in the vehicles where they were invited and welcomed.

The Professor led the way, wisely choosing to follow the fence over the rough ground, rather than the road around the marsh. Two hours later, without any serious bother, they arrived at Paddy's Bore, for a late lunch. The Professor made it clear that this was just a "dinner time camp"; Brolga Springs was their aim.

Soon after their arrival, Clinton was able to report where they were to Hugh and Gwen, who were still searching along the track to the coast.

"Hugh," Gwen turned on her smile, "Can we go back to Paddy's Bore. I want to talk to Natasha, Annie and Tracey while they prepare and eat their lunchtime meal. I have been neglecting the women's angle on these events lately." Hugh thought she put a very strong case,

"Ok." he agreed. "If we didn't find Quealey and his mate, the other blokes probably didn't either. We might have another look this afternoon."

So both helicopters were back at Paddy's Bore in time for another of Annie's lunches, Sam wishing to get away from the Corporation men and rejoin Tracey in his own vehicle. He felt that he had been wasting some of their precious time.

The Corporation men found that they were hungry enough to eat a share of Annie's cooking. Gwen was busy showing everyone where the lost Japanese had camped in their limestone cave; Sam joined in showing the signs of where there were goannas, wallabies and lizards they could have caught and eaten. Annie added her bit,

"Plenty berries and bush tucker here, that mob stupid to starve." Clinton Strong made the suggestion that he would drive a short way down the track towards Kununurra to see if he could find the two Japanese still not tracked down. Hugh considered this idea for a while, finally agreeing if one of the bush vehicles also went with him.

This could not be arranged, they all wanted to go to Brolga Springs and set up camp.

"We can find those stupid Japs just as easy tomorrow on our way home!" grumbled Punch, summing up the general feeling. Preparations for the drive to Brolga Springs began.

CHAPTER FIVE.
THE BROLGA SPRING'S CAMP.

Finishing their lunch, Hugh, Sam, Punch and the Professor conferred over their cup of tea. They chewed over the probabilities, death from exhaustion or heat stroke, drowning in the creek, a misunderstanding with a crocodile. It seemed unlikely that the problem could be solved from the air, it was decided to fly one more time, then a ground party would have to go and look.

Gwen and Hugh wanted to try again; Gwen of course wanted her story. The Corporation men made it obvious that they were to continue their search; the Professor reluctantly agreed to go with them instead of Sam.

Punch and Sam got to work to get their vehicles and gear ready to move on.

They would camp for a day or so at Brolga Springs, there was shelter available in the sheds and the house. Sergeant Clinton Strong was to be the only soldier to remain with Hugh, the two drivers made it clear that they wished to go home.

The renewed search for the two missing men was brief and fruitless.

Both helicopters had to leave for Kununurra to refuel, taking the last of the Norforce detailed R & R soldiers with them.

Hugh, Gwen and the Professor had returned to Paddy's Bore in time to lead the procession of vehicles to Brolga Springs. The two places are only a few miles apart, but the track is blacksoil. There were many pools of water remaining on the track after the cyclone storms, winches were needed and it was mid-afternoon by the time they arrived to set up camp at Brolga Springs.

Parking their vehicles, everyone set about cleaning out the abandoned tin house; it still had benches, sink and taps, wash tub, shower and toilet, but no water supply. Annie was the boss of the cleaning, showing the girls how to wrap a bunch of leafy branches with wire to make a broom, and how to use it;

"Come on you girls, we got to get this place respectable." It soon was, it dared not be!

Sam set about the water problem; he went down the slope to the bore, found the tap that fed water to the house tank, turned it on and went back to the tank. Presently the water arrived, as the mill slowly pumped with the early afternoon sea breeze. Sam was disgusted to see it run straight out of the holes in the lower sides of the tank.

"The bloody things rusted out!"

He looked about, found some old clothes used for cleaning rags in the workshop shed and with the help of BBC and Bruce, set about mending the water tank. Standing on top of a Toyota, they were able to partly block the holes so that the tank held some of the water. Natasha, Lesley and Jane watched this repair, they were waiting for turns in the shower.

"Can we drink this water?" Lesley wanted to know, "Those bits of cloth in the holes don't look very clean." BBC spluttered and walked away, leaving Sam to answer;

"After a while the water inside will be clean, see how much water is getting out, it will have the dirt in it, the water inside will soon be clean enough to drink. You can boil it to make sure if you wish, but it is good enough for me as it is."

He climbed back up to Bruce with more rags and bits of stick; they poked and mended, reducing the flow. Concentrating on plugging up one hole, Bruce accidentally bumped one of the sticks in place in a hole nearby. The stick was dislodged, it burst out together with the cloth it was holding in place and another piece of the rotting tank.

Sam found he was in the wrong place at the wrong time. The stick, the rag and the bit of the tank caught him squarely in the face. He retreated saturated, disgruntled with the mirth that his misfortune aroused in the onlookers. Sam was a good target for amusement, given his customary solemn bearing. Bruce worked on, stifling his amused chuckles, until he was satisfied that the tank would hold enough water.

The tap over the wash tub would not turn off, they found another on a stand in the garden that worked, screwed it off, blocked the pipe with a plug of wood and put the tap in place over the wash tub; they solved the problems one by one until there was enough water in the tank and everything they needed worked. Soon there was water for drinking and washing and for showers for everyone

That night at the new Brolga Springs camp was a happy gathering of friends. Everyone was pleased with what they had done that day, and the stories of each of their doings were told with mirth and goodwill. The only regrets were the news of the finding of more bodies in the Boeing and the failure to find the unlamented Lang Harte-Quealey III and his companion. The big Bell helicopter had come back to the wreck from it's trip to Kununurra and the morgue people had had more bodies unearthed for them.

Second Officer Eric Peng had had a hard day. He had arrived at the camp at sunset, having persuaded the pilot of the Bell to drop him off on their way to Kununurra.

"First I had the Airline men, they wanted me to tell them all about the storm, what happened to the Boeing, why we landed here, questions, questions, questions, my head was ringing, I hope I told them everything properly." He was worried that anything he might have said might be bad for the Captain and First Officer, who, he said, were still in Darwin Hospital.

"Then," he continued, "All the bodies had to be taken away. We had to count them all first. That was terrible, the smell, I was sick many times, but no matter how often we counted, we could not get the numbers right." He looked at Annie,

"My belly has been empty all day, can you fill it for me with some supper?" Annie gave him her broad smile, his was one plate sure to be full.

"They found four more bodies buried deep in the mud in the cargo hold," he looked at Tracey;

"That was why there was such a bad smell when we were there last evening. I got away from there as soon as I could. It is much better here in your camp." After a pause, Eric continued;

"When Nugget made his list, there were nine names short, compared to the passenger manifest, after allowing for the five Americans, the eleven Japanese and the bodies we knew about." He paused to accept a whisky and water. The Professor had liberated eight more bottles, there were still some left, hidden in the scrub.

"We should have found nineteen bodies at the tail of the Boeing, we only found seventeen. That crocodile must have taken two." Eric gave an involuntary shudder, along with most of his listeners.

"By the names of the passengers who should have been sitting close to where the wall blew out, and the names we think we have for the bodies, there could have been as many as three passengers sucked out by the decompression." Shudders all around again, rum and whisky steadied nerves.

"That still leaves two passengers for which we cannot account at all."

"Then the investigator men, the government men, they want to know everything all again. I tell them what I can, I am sick of talking, I tell them. I have a bad day, you might be sick of me talking now, someone else can talk." To his astonishment he was rewarded by a round of applause. They all liked Eric, he was a good, caring, sociable man, always ready to help, he would be missed when he had to leave.

Tracey, when she had finally got out of bed, unable to stand all the helicopter noise, had spent the morning with Annie and the girls.

"For a little time", she reported, "I sat and talked with Natasha. She told me all about her mining city of Mount Isa. I am to go with her to that place one day."

Sam lifted his eyebrows, but wisely said nothing.

"Annie took us for a "bogey" in her pool, again. That was fun. It was lovely to be able to wash our hair again." She then gently embarrassed some of the girls by telling swimming pool tales out of school. Tracey got a round of applause also.

Gwen had her say, sipping on her whisky,

"In the afternoon, when we went for a second look for Mr. Harte-Quealey, we flew low over the track, and landed quite a few times, looking for footprints, and under big trees or dense clumps of bushes. We found some traces of footprints, but they did not tell us much. We could not search for long, both helicopters had to go for fuel. It is a pity that we do not have a few drums of fuel here"

"When are they coming back?" Punch wanted to know, he had not been for a ride in one yet.

"Mine will come and get me when I want it, or to collect reports," Gwen responded, "But I cannot tell you about the Harte-Quealey Corporation one. From what the Professor and I heard, those two blokes are in disgrace, some other big shot is coming sometime tomorrow to show them how it is done, he has promised to find our Mr. Harte-Quealey without fail."

"Good on him, bewdy!" put in Sam, who had had more than enough of the Corporation men.

Gwen still had the floor.

"I want to come with you blokes in your wagons tomorrow, and for the next few days. We still have to find the rest of the Japanese as well as the other two Americans. I've had a long talk this afternoon with my bosses through the radio link, I am to work for a few days, then have a two week holiday." She turned to look at Hugh, this was news to him. Finding everybody looking at him, grinning, he went a deep red, then busied himself inspecting the bottom of his whiskey mug.

"I'll get even with that lovely bitch!" he promised himself, never the less delighted at the news.

"Now," continued Gwen, "More news. If there were more people here I would get you all to stand in the middle while we cheered, but there would only be about three of us to do the cheering. It seems you are all bloody heroes, you are to be given a civic reception when you get back to Kununurra, the passengers have made a big fuss of you. So I'm staying to do your story."

Unlike the previous speakers, Gwen did not get applause. They were too stunned. Punch seemed pleased, he was, after all, the showman of the group, but there were serious murmurs of fright.

"Jeeze," said Sam, "I'm going fishing at Tanmurra for a month!" The others sat thinking it through. Annie gave a giggle.

"Think of all the free drinks we'll get!" That thought stopped Punch in his tracks.

"Reckon we might go fishing with Sam," he growled, looking at Annie. Chantelle looked at the Professor. He looked carefully back, but said nothing.

In the silence that followed, Clinton Strong took the floor.

"We got all the bodies flown out," he said, "and the three Americans, after they were patched up and fed." He turned to the Professor.

"We sent your mate Rabbit off too; he went with four bodies, four soldiers and the seven Japanese. He didn't seem too happy." The Professor nodded.

"We have finished here now, except for helping you mob look for the rest of the Japanese and the two Americans. Four of our Landrovers are packed up and waiting at Yow Springs to be collected later" He turned to look at Sam and Hugh. They made no comment.

Lance Park then spoke up for the footballers and the art tour ladies.

"There are only four of us left, Harry Green, Jane Burrows, Lesley Roberts and myself," he indicated each one as he spoke, almost like an introduction.

"We have all been very happy living and working with you all, and would like to stay." He turned to look at Eric.

"Eric says we must go tomorrow, we should have gone today. We have all been trying to be useful, getting firewood and helping with the cooking. We badly need some clean or new clothes, but really just want to stay with you people" This also got a round of applause. Hugh looked at Eric, they both looked at the Professor, but nothing was then said.

Punch now had his say, looking at the Professor.

"I stayed to make sure that Rabbit was flown out, I told him what you said about getting out of the Kimberley. He reckons you are a hard man, but he is frightened of you now, he'll keep going." He looked around, with a broad grin,

"You must have given him a couple of good wallops, the poor bastard couldn't sit down!" Punch laughed aloud, joined by the camp as he related how Rabbit did not want to sit when he got into the helicopter.

"You should have seen the look on his dial when they made him!" laughed Punch. The general laughter at this died away suddenly when they saw the look on Natasha's face. She sat solemn for a short time and then buried her face in Chantelle's lap. The conversation turned suddenly to the program for tomorrow, as Annie and her helpers began to serve food.

By consent it was finally agreed that the fencers and bullcatchers would move out at dawn and thoroughly search the track to the coast. Hugh elected to go along with this party in his Army vehicle, and invited

Gwen to go with him. Once the two Americans were found, the searchers could concentrate on the track south for the missing Japanese as they went down it on their way to Kununurra.

What to do with the two unofficial honeymooner couples, the footballers and their partners? Everyone liked them, they were welcome to stay, but would this be allowed? Much discussion, much conjecture. Hugh summed it all up.

"You can stay until someone demands you be flown out, we won't remind them that you are here. Gwen can get some fresh clothes, toilet gear and whatever sent up for you in her helicopter. You are responsible if anything goes wrong, be it on your own heads. Officially we told you to go, but you refused. Is that all ok?"

"That'll do us," chorused the four, beaming all around.

It was then decided that, as a group, they would help the Corporation Jet Ranger helicopter if it turned up, but, as Sam said,

"I hope the bastards keep well away!"

Eight bottles of good wine and spirits shared around, with some who were very light drinkers, led to a late, noisy and merry night, before all the swags were rolled out, be they proper canvas or just bundles of blankets.

Quiet had scarcely settled on the camp when a gentle rain began to fall. Those with swags outdoors made a quiet scuttle for shelter in shed or house.

It was into a very wet and dewy morning that, long before sunrise, the Professor was able to untangle himself and emerge from his swag. He did not know which clung tighter, the sheet, Chantelle or the mossie net. He found that Punch was also up, with Annie rousing herself.

Once the fire got going, everyone started to appear, the smell of tea, toast and coffee was too much. The Professor sat, yarning to Punch and BBC, eating toast and drinking tea. They were content, the world was good.

The Professor wandered down the slope to sit on a large tea tree branch, one which ran parallel to the ground, making a convenient seat. He liked to sit here when visiting Brolga Springs, it gave a great view out over the marsh, and you could almost see the sea. After a time Natasha came and sat close to him, turning to look into his face.

"Are you going to keep Chantelle?" she asked. The professor was a little thrown.

"She is not mine to keep," he said slowly.

"You mean she's going back to that lousy Sam?" she asked.

"No, I know she's not going to do that."

"Well, why don't you keep her, she wants you?"

"I can't do that, she's a young girl, she should find a good man and marry him, not get tied up with an old bloke like me."

"She doesn't want to get married, she wants a bloke like Sam, but not him, so she can come and go, not proper married!" She spoke scornfully, as if everyone should know that.

They sat for a while, quiet, both thinking.

"What do you want?" she finally asked.

"Me, I have a wife already, so what do I want?" he asked back.

"You could have a girlfriend as well, on the secret," she turned to face him, "You did with Annie!" He shifted uncomfortably.

"Who told you that?"

"Everyone knows."

"Well, I don't want to do it again; it causes too much trouble, and is not fair to anyone."

"Chantelle is waiting for you, she wants you to be her "secret", you can keep her if you want. Maybe you don't like her?" She turned and looked hopefully at him. The Professor had no time to prepare his reply;

"Do you want me?" she asked, in the direct way that caught him off guard.

"Christ!" he muttered to himself, inaudibly, "What do I say now?" As he looked in utter confusion into that beaming smile, he was saved by the approaching footsteps of Chantelle, who had a mug of tea and a slice of buttered toast for him. As he drank the tea both girls sat without speaking, side by side on the branch with him. It was too much, he gulped hot tea, burning his mouth, spluttered;

"I've got to get ready for the search, we have to leave soon!" Drained the last of his drink and bolted.

CHAPTER SIX.

CUTHBERT LANGFORD
HARTE-QUEALEY III.

ALONG WITH Eric, Hugh, Gwen and Punch, the Professor had unpacked his Toyota the night before, putting stores and gear in the shed down the slope. This left the three vehicles ready for an early start to set off on the search to the coast. Gwen's crew travelled with her and Hugh.

"Tell you what," commented the Professor just before they left, "I've been thinking. They probably got right to the coast, that lady, Helen Anderson, said they had a long walk back when they got away from their boss, we should go to the coast and work back." Nobody disputed that, they all wanted to get to the seashore anyway.

An hour later, without too many wet, boggy patches on the track delaying them, they came out of the scrub on top of a small headland, with a rocky shore line in front, the Timor Sea breaking over the rocks below. To the left a small creek ran into the sea over a little sandbank on a beach that ran, gentle waves rolling in, several kilometres west to a broken rocky headland. The rocks of that headland were broken into tall pillars, running in a line from Shakespeare Hill inland out into the water, the feature known as "The Needles."

Blue was the colour, a misty blue tinted the vast ocean in front of them and the white sand of the beach; it gave The Needles a purplish plum colour. Even the rocks just below the headland were slightly bluish.

To the east another beach, silver and white, curved away as far as the eye could see. The only jarring note was the rubbish and junk, the flattened grass and bushes left behind by the regulars who camped on the headland most weekends in the dry season, fishing or just sitting and looking, drink in hand.

The Professor left his vehicle and led the way on foot to the water, over the rocky shelf. It was sandstone, bearing intricate coloured strata patterns through its entire width. Very soon everyone was picking up loose bits of the flat rock, admiring the patterns. The object of their search was temporarily forgotten, they were diverted by the attractions of this bit of the coast.

Arriving at the creek side of the shore, they found the tide at the right height to be washing in and out of a number of very small rock pools.

"Last one in cooks the lunch", was the cry as the Professor showed the way.

"What about sharks and crocs?" Gwen was nervous.

"There's only room for me in this pool, and if one of those blokes wants to come in, I'll see him a mile away. And if he thinks I'll move over, just now, he's in for a fight, I'll kick his head in. Russell Coight move over!" The Professor finished on a high note.

He settled his rump more comfortably on a "soft" rock, prepared to spend some time in the cold, salty spa-like pool. He needed a good salt soak, he considered. Gwen look at the picture of the men, hats on, stripped to stubbies or shorts, perched on their rocks in their separate pools as the waves rocked them about. The camera rolled again with a dripping operator. Gwen then joined the men, modestly still in her shorts and top.

Some time later a drip-drying Professor emerged, refreshed, to direct the areas for each to search.

"Don't get lost, stay in sight of the track or the creek and each other, don't go too far, the two we are looking for would have done just that, I think, keeping close to the water."

They wandered off in their given directions. They did not have to search for long, suddenly there was a yell from Punch,

"There's a bloke sitting under that tree!" He stood watching the slumped, immobile figure of a man, as the others gathered. He was not far from where the vehicles were parked, had the searchers looked about on arrival they would possibly seen him then. Cuthbert Langford Harte-Quealey III sat hunched, his back to the trunk of a pandanus tree, unmindful of the spines, looking out over the creek. His gaze was fixed on the sandy beach opposite and the sea beyond. He did not seem to be aware of the people gathering around him. He was muddy, scratched and bleeding, sunburnt through his ragged clothes, his face scarlet and peeling, not at all the picture of the big tycoon. He also had a long, open slashed wound down the outside of his right thigh. He sat there placidly, ignoring the flies that were making a meal of his wounds. He was a very ordinary sight, for an esteemed tycoon.

"Are you sure that's the bloke we're looking for?" asked Punch doubtfully, he didn't want to be robbed of finding the right fellow. Eric looked closely, the man sitting there did not respond.

"I can't be sure, but it must be him, it's not the other man who was with him." Eric and Gwen took the hands of the man and tried to get him to stand. He did not respond, they could not lift him.

"He's a zombie," said Punch. "He did not even see us drive up."

Gwen looked thoughtful;

"He was probably sitting there yesterday, when we flew around, too hard for us to see, sitting still. We were looking for someone who would run out and wave his arms about." Eric came back with a cup of water. After an effort they got Lang to drink some of it. The camera rolled.

Hugh and Punch got a fire going;

"Have to make him some soup, we can have an early lunch, anyway," observed Hugh. They put up a tarpaulin between two of the wagons for shade, the headland was a bit bare of shade trees and then the men carried the unresponsive Lang into its shelter. He suddenly crawled until he could see the creek and the beach beyond, then leant back, in an almost coma-like state, against the wheel of a 4WD. While he was sitting quietly, Gwen took the opportunity to examine his long thigh and leg wound. Under her guidance, and against some resistance from Lang, they used sea water to clean and dress his raw wound, covering it as best they could to keep the flies away. His numerous smaller wounds and scratches were also cleaned.

While the others were cooking or occupied dressing Lang's wounds, Sam and the Professor were very interested in the large leg wound, quietly speculating as to what may have caused it. They each had a theory, but did not agree, so they did not share their ideas with the others.

By the time the dressings were completed their meal was ready. As they ate, they took it in turns to slowly feed warm soup to the gaunt figure. Discussion arose as to what they were to do with this new patient.

Then engine noises turned their attention to the sky, the Corporate hired helicopter landed in a blast of sand, guided in by Sam on the ground.

Gwen, ever perceptive to the possibility of a story, had her camera man already filming.

The new big boss did not waste time. The helicopter was scarcely on the ground before he strode across, as was the habit of Corporation men, dispensing with greetings or introductions.

"Who's this?" he demanded, indicating the figure of Lang. "Why are you wasting time with him?,

"We think he's your boss," Punch observed dryly. The remark, for a time, went right over the head of the new boss, who was looking around, apparently puzzled, at the inactive group.

"What?" he suddenly exclaimed, looking at the man for the first time. He crouched down, examining the face closely.

"Holy Mother, it is him," he rose to his feet,

"What have you done to him?" he demanded in a shout.

"You people should have found him sooner and looked after him properly. How did he get into this state? As soon as we get to the lawyers he'll have you people sorted out." The shouting was set to continue, but Sam was equal to the occasion, he moved his large, muscled bushman's body directly in front of the Corporation man.

"Now, before you get too excited, let's get a few things straight. If that is your boss, we did all we could to find him as soon as we could. We found him before you did!" He looked at the cameraman.

"You got that on film?" There was a nod of confirmation.

"Now see that fire? My mates have made him soup, carried him here into the shade, given him water, and looked after him." The corporation man took a step back, looking a little doubtful in the face of the obvious hostility of the whole group.

"Now there is another thing I want you to know, and for you to tell us here and now, on tape. Anything that has happened to this silly bugger here, this fool your boss," pointing his thumb, "He did to himself. Is that right?" The post-hole boring eyes went to work. The corporation man was not happy,

"Yes, I agree," he spluttered, "It was his idea to leave the crash."

Sam continued;

"Are you going to stand around abusing us, or are you concerned enough about your boss to arrange help for him? And to find his mate?" Sam again indicated the still running camera, taping it all.

"What do you want to do now?" asked Hugh, "we are still trying to feed him. And we have yet to find Steve Roper"

"Who the hell is Steve Roper?" The Corporation boss was dismissive.

"He is the only one of Lang's party who we have not yet found. Aren't you concerned about him?"

"You can find him later, he should have taken better care of Lang. We have to get him out of here at once." Gwen took her opportunity.

"You are only concerned to get Lang lifted out, you don't care about Steve?" The Corporation man had already forgotten the camera.

"Roper can be found later, we are wasting time, are you people going to help me?" The rescuers looked to the Professor and to Sam for guidance.

"He's a sick man, so we have to help him. We are only doing it for him, if you were both well we wouldn't lift a finger. What do you want to do?" Sam was scathing in his response.

"We can fly straight to Kununurra, to the hospital, he can be treated there. Can you help me get him in?"

They found that this was not an easy task. The creature who had been Cuthbert Langford Harte-Quealey III was content to sit placidly when looking out over the creek to the beach and the ocean, but he became very agitated when he was moved from looking at this view. He had to be forcibly placed into a seat in the helicopter and his hands had to be tied so that he could not undo his seat belt. This treatment caused him to make a series of bleating roars in protest, a noise that was very unpleasant. The Corporation boss and his pilot were already showing signs of distress as they belted themselves in for takeoff.

Within minutes the helicopter swooped out over the sea, swung around to the left and headed south. The small group settled quietly down, subdued and thoughtful, to continue with their lunch. Punch summed up their thoughts;

"Money isn't everything," he observed to no one in particular. No one was prepared to comment, reflectively eating in silence, sipping their hot tea.

Not so Hugh and Gwen, they were busy on the radio, to the SES in Kununurra.

"We have found Harte-Quealey," Gwen told them, "His people are flying him to the hospital in Kununurra. Can you please send a message to my producer, I need my helicopter urgently, the pilot can find us on the track from Brolga Springs to the Coast. We have not yet found any trace of Steve Roper, or the two missing Japanese."

The pictures of the rescue of Lang and his condition would be international news by that night.

Their lunch concluded, Sam joined the searchers as they carefully block searched the whole area. They did not find any trace of Steve Roper. It took them all afternoon; they examined every inch of the land on every side of the headland, and carefully all along the beach and rocks at low tide.

Satisfied that there was no trace of Steve Roper on their side of the creek, Sam and the Professor stood looking across the creek to the beach on the other side.

"Have you got your rifle here with you?" Sam asked.

"Why, what do you want to do?"

"We haven't looked at all on the other side of this creek." Sam shifted uneasily and continued. "That bloke Lang could not take his eyes off that beach. It looked to me that he badly wanted to get over there, but knew he could not."

"Have you got a plan to go over there?" the Professor inquired.

"No, not yet, but you bring your rifle and we'll have a look about."

Without attracting any attention from the other members of the search party, the Professor collected his .22 Magnum from his Toyota and rejoined Sam on the bank of the creek.

"The only place that seems practical to cross is where that pool back there spills over the bank to run down to the sea. Wherever we choose to cross there is a current and the water is deep enough to make wading through a problem." Sam was well aware of the dangers of crossing the creek. Where the water ran down to enter the sea, the creek bottom was loose sand. Wading over there was not possible, the current would undermine the sand and a wader would loose his footing.

"A man would soon be shark bait if he went in there." was the Professor's opinion. "The only place that I can see to cross is on the sea edge of that pool, that rim seems to be solid, the water is slow moving there. It's deep enough to be a bit of a worry, though."

They moved up the creek to have a better look. The pool was still and dark, covered in water weeds, growing thick and covering it's surface, right up to the rim. This rim or edge of the pool appeared to be rock, with rough edges, smoothed over with stable sand. The two men eyed it carefully, with considerable nervousness and suspicion.

"Are you sure you still want to go over there?" The professor was not at all pleased with the idea.

"Think I'll give it a go." Sam did not sound too happy, either, but it was his idea and he felt he had to go on with it.

"You be close behind me and keep that bloody rifle cocked and ready. I don't think a shark would be up here, but that pool looks like a good croc. home to me."

Sam led the way as they started to wade across the creek, cautiously feeling his way, being careful to keep his footing in the sand. A very concerned Professor followed, alert for whatever might happen.

Suddenly the surface of the weed covered pool burst open as a large crocodile lunged, jaws wide, towards Sam. Immediately the Professor began to shoot, straight into the open jaws. As Sam, handicapped by the water, yelling loudly for help, desperately tried to get away, the Professor fired shot after shot into that gaping mouth, an action which saved Sam as the lunging crocodile slowed, snapping it's jaws closed just inches from him. A .22 Magnum is high powered, but the projectile is not very large. It took a number of shots before the crocodile reacted, slowing down and not being close enough to fasten onto Sam. Despite the bullets, the animal charged again, slamming its jaws shut in the face of a furiously back pedalling Sam. It then swung back to disappear under the weeds. Sam came rapidly floundering towards the Professor and splashed past, gasping for air as he reached the bank. The Professor, backing away with his rifle at the ready, retreated carefully to the safety of the edge of the creek and then turned to join Sam.

Sam's first words were to thank the Professor for his protection.

"You did good, mate, when that big bastard came at me I thought I was a goner," he gasped.

"I didn't do all that well, the bugger got away." The Professor was apologetic. Suddenly he rounded on Sam, exclaiming:

"We've got to be a couple of prize Rambos! Why did we have to try to wade over that creek when all we had to do was wait for Gwen's helicopter to carry us over?" Sam looked long and carefully at the Professor.

"Now you tell me!" His only response.

They moved slowly together, over to the shade of a small tree. Sam was still gasping for air. They sat to recover as all the other members of the search party came running. Those who were close had heard the shots over the surf noise, the others just followed. There were many nervous looks and back-pedalling away from the dark, weedy pool as Sam and the Professor, still gasping from lack of air and fright, quietly told them what had happened.

Although she did not say it, Gwen was clearly regretful that Sam and the Professor had not let her film crew know of their aborted ill-fated plan to cross the creek. Ever the reporter, the crocodile would have made great filming, she thought. It did, very briefly, cross her mind to ask them for a re-run, but wisely she immediately abandoned such an idea.

"Well, that winds it up for me, I want to go back to Brolga Springs." Punch voiced the opinion of them all.

The search party was still packing up to leave when Gwen's helicopter found them.

Sam and the Professor hitched a ride on it to the other side of the creek, where they searched thoroughly without result.

Some food stores and fresh bread were delivered, the tapes Gwen had were collected, and then away the helicopter went, in a hurry to get to Kununurra and to avoid the large storm that the pilot reported was developing to the south.

As the searchers on the ground prepared to drive off the Professor spoke;

"I don't believe this place will ever be the same for me." Sam looked across;

"Are you kidding, I'm never coming here again." No one else made any comment.

It was late afternoon as they drove away from Ribbon Rock Point; as they drove they continued to look at all the places in which a person could be concealed back along the whole track to Brolga Springs; no sign of their man.

Steve Roper had disappeared.

CHAPTER SEVEN.
LAST NIGHT AT BROLGA SPRINGS.

I T IS a universal truth that housework is inescapable. Gather two or more people in a camp or a house, meals have to be prepared and cooked, fires or stoves made ready, potatoes peeled, knives, forks and plates and bowls cleaned and stored. Annie was a fast and efficient worker, but even she needed helpers. True, she had Judy, Chantelle and Natasha, but they combined were not enough. It did not help that Annie was more than a little jealous of Chantelle and suspicious of Natasha. Mutual distrust did not lead to efficient co-operation at times.

It did not take Annie long to put the two girls, Jane Burrows and Leslie Roberts to work. They were happy with this; they got on well with Annie, her stories and antics kept them amused all day. Annie was a good boss, well able to make her wishes clear, even if her "Creole" or broken English had them confused sometimes. Jane and Leslie also, unconsciously, perhaps, acted as a foil between Annie, Chantelle and Natasha.

Annie was a woman of the world, if she had not seen it all, she had seen most. Coupled with a good memory, Annie could tell a story of most events, almost always very basic, risqué to the point of crudeness if she chose. This was a new world to Jane and Leslie, they were sceptical of Annie's stories in the beginning, but her obvious sincerity and consistent themes won them over. They could also get confirmation from Judy.

The footballers, Lance and Harry were also given jobs. Heavy things to carry, firewood to collect, Annie did not let them rest for long. "BBC" and Bruce also needed their help, butchering a beast, hanging the meat

40

away from the flies, supplying the cuts that Annie needed. It cannot be said that they enjoyed all the jobs that they were given, but their ladies were never far away, and this kept them very happy.

Despite having the cleaned up house at Brolga Springs in which to prepare their meals, the lack of a stove meant that an outdoor fireplace was still necessary. With their usual flair, and the good supply of food to choose from, Annie and her helpers had a feast ready that evening. It was served outside, the house not having any furniture. The meal was eaten early, in deference to the threatening weather. Annie rounded her diners up promptly.

"If youse blokes don't come and eat now, the rain will get you, and I'm not going to get wet again if you're late."

The rain she referred to had been building up all afternoon. The search party had watched the storm away to the south, as they worked their way back to Brolga Springs. Sam and the Professor had continually looked at it, closely, speculating that it might wet the track to the south, and hold them up tomorrow.

"Can't be sure," observed the Professor, "But I think it is mostly to the west of the road. It should not bother us, the way it is, but it could come up here, or move east."

At the conclusion of Annie's early supper, the Professor produced the last four bottles from Eric's supply, from some mysterious place under the stores in his Toyota. Toasts were drunk, and stories again told. The first of these was to Sam and the Professor for their escape from the crocodile. Sam was given an extra glass, as Punch said, to steady his nerves. (With Tracey at his side, Sam thought she could make all the "steadiness" that he currently wanted.) Everyone had something to say about the crocodile escapade; the two were congratulated on their escape many times, coupled with a ration of derision for not having waited for the helicopter to cross the creek.

Gwen then held the floor with two stories from her media contacts, tales that set the tone for a happy "last night" party. It was obvious that Tracey, Eric and the two honeymoon couples, perhaps Gwen and her crew, would have to leave next day.

"You remember that Japanese bridegroom who left his new bride behind at the crash to go look for a town?" began Gwen, "Well, to his absolute astonishment and complete loss of face, when he got to Darwin he found she was back in Japan." Gwen went on, "The Japanese media is making much of the story, it seems the poor girl wants nothing further to do with him."

"My other story is a very happy one," Gwen went on, "You all remember Nugget, Adelaide and the baby we called "Mudlark"? Well, when they got to Darwin the welfare people wanted to take the baby into their care, until her relatives could be found. Adelaide and Nugget objected, they had formed a strong attachment to her, the baby was happy and responding well to them."

Gwen had their full attention, they all liked and respected Nugget and Adelaide.

"Nothing further has so far been found out about the mother and baby. It is assumed she used a false address and details to get away from someone, perhaps a husband or boy friend. Her passport is genuine, it is quite new, and all the addresses given for it were box numbers or false. So no one has claimed the baby."

"Now when the welfare people came to the hotel to collect her, all of Nugget's footballers still in Darwin, the Arts tour girls, and dozens of the passengers, with the media, were there to stop them. There was quite a protest, threats of arrest, all the usual fuss, but "Mudlark" is still with Nugget and Adelaide."

Gwen was pleased, her listeners gave a round of applause.

"It is early days yet; the NT Minister has agreed to let "Mudlark" stay with her new "family" for the present. Adelaide and Nugget have decided to get married and then apply formally to adopt "Mudlark", they now call her Kimberley, and will make this her proper name." Gwen was pleased with the reaction to her news, but even she was surprised at the reaction to her next item.

"Adelaide and Nugget say they will get married in Kununurra, so you can all be at the wedding. They reckon that the footballers and art ladies can all do with a trip to the Kimberley, so the whole rescue mob can get together again." There were loud cheers from the group, and an excited chatter followed.

After things settled down again, Lance Park led Jane Burrows by the hand to stand in the middle of the group.

"We're going to get married too!" he blurted out, to Jane's blushes. "Just as soon as we can. You are all invited." Turning to Gwen, he burst out;

"We don't wish to go yet, our work here isn't finished, and we want to stay."

Jane tugged him back to the edge of the crowd.

"What about Leslie and Harry?" Annie wanted to know. There was no response, but a couple in the shadows held each other tightly. Gwen left the group, and got busy on her radio. She was soon back, her news left them all a little sad. Her helicopter had come early in the afternoon to collect her film of the finding of Cuthbert Langford Harte-Quealey III, bringing in fresh clothes for the ladies, soaps and toilet gear. It was now to do two trips in the morning, to take Jane, Lance, Lesley and Harry back to Kununurra. The airline and the rescue people were insisting they had to go. However, Eric and Tracey were requested to stay with the group until the missing Japanese were found. From tomorrow Gwen was on holidays.

There was a general movement towards sleeping bags and shelters. There was a great variety of these, Lance and Harry had made up swags from torn up tarpaulins, blankets and mosquito nets scrounged from the Army blokes. Eric had similar gear, while Tracey and Gwen slept in the respective swags of Sam and Hugh.

Gwen, Hugh, the Professor and Sam remained behind, conversing in low tones.

"You remember that long slash down the leg of that Lang bloke?" Sam was saying, "Well, do you reckon that croc. of mine might have made it for him?"

Hugh and Gwen looked surprised, then very interested. The Professor had been chewing over his thoughts on the subject since Sam's escape, but decided not to reach any unproven conclusion.

"It might be that the crocodile did have a go at him, but we really don't know what may have happened." The others all spoke at once.

"That's it, it must have been that crocodile!"

"You may be right, but if it was, how did he get away? That bloke would hang on, Lang and Steve had no weapons, you saw how determined it was to grab Sam, even with bullets hitting it." They stood looking at him, thinking that over. After a pause, the Professor continued.

"Now don't any of you get carried away. I know Steve Roper has disappeared, but none of you were there or have any evidence as to what may have happened. What we do know is that Lang could not take his eyes off that beach on the other side of the creek, and that something dramatic must have taken place to render him so traumatised." The other three were not so content with this view; they all had their theories, but agreed to settle for the Professor's advice.

"Think what you want, but remember, those Corporation blokes have mobs of legal blokes and the money to pay them. If they think that you might be maligning Lang, expect a nasty visit from them, and the prospect of spending a lot of money."

The subject, except for very private observations amongst themselves, remained closed.

Sam had his wagon down the slope under a tree, Lance had a blanket bed rigged up in the shed, Natasha had her swag safely in the front seat of the Professors truck, Hugh was parked at the back of the house, the little camps were spread about. All set for an interesting night. Thing was, though, the storm did not see it that way. Within half an hour it was blowing a gale, wind and dust everywhere. Mossie nets were down, tarps unfastened, and big raindrops started to fall. There was a rush into the house and shed for shelter. Privacy disappeared. Sam was disgruntled, but there was nothing he could do about it. He was particularly disappointed, as since his escape from the crocodile Tracey had been very attentive to him.

Despite this, the weather made it easy for Tracey to follow her mother's instructions that night.

Punch and Annie had rigged their mosquito net over their swag under one of the larger trees well down the slope away from the house and shed. This big tree sheltered them from the storm for a few minutes; they did not wake up until it was getting well wound up. As soon as he was aware of the heavy rain Punch rolled Annie out of the swag, grabbed it in a bundle and set out for the shelter of the shed.

When Annie untangled herself from the mosquito net Punch was well on his way, she galloped after him, the wind and rain lashing her bare body. They were fortunate in that the shed was not lit, otherwise those already there would have been treated to the hilarious sight of a naked Punch, clutching his bedding, pursued by an indignant and shouting Annie, her naked body streaming with rain. It was some time before they settled down in their damp swag, Annie not being one to hide her displeasure.

The storm was the usual ten to fifteen minutes of fury, followed by very heavy rain for a time. After being forced to shift camp out of the rain, with wet swags and blankets, the searchers and romantics did not sleep well. Disappointment may have added to the gloom of some. This made for a damp and gloomy camp that next early morning at Brolga Springs.

Punch was up early, his hands around a mug of tea, he watched with interest as the Professor got himself out of his early morning tangle.

"We must be getting soft," he observed, to the Professor and anyone else around;

"A little bit of a storm has us all running for shelter. A few days ago we were in the rain all the time. What's wrong with you mob?" He got little response, just glum looks.

Annie was, as usual, starting to cook on the fire Punch had helped her start. The smell of coffee and frying was too much, even down the slope in the shed they could smell it. Sam sat up and looked around, his wagon was parked half into the shed; other couples were emerging from their blankets. Despite the sun which was shining in long low yellow beams under the last of the storm cloud, he was not happy. He looked at Tracey, a small neat figure under the blanket, still half asleep.

"Does a bloke have to marry her, to make love to her?" he mused to himself. It seemed the answer was "Yes!" Sam did not know if he could bring himself to ask such a question, nor could he be certain that the answer would also be "Yes." The fencer was not happy with complications he could not solve, he was a bull at the gate man, but he had enough sense to know that this would not work with Tracey. He told himself he had some serious thinking to do, he got up and went to get some breakfast for the two of them, something he had never done in his life before.

Tracey, lying awake with her eyes closed, opened them to watch him leave. She knew she was in love with this big man, but did she want to marry him?

"I'll have to talk to mother about him," she told herself, "She will know what I should do." She was proud of the fact that she had kept Sam in check, and glad that he had no idea how close she had come once or twice to giving in. She shuddered, in the light of day she realised how easy it would have been. It was nice, as a cabin attendant, to have someone bring her breakfast, even if it was all heaped here and there on the one plate, toast, fried meat, butter and a pool of jam. As women have realised for centuries, it is the thought that counts.

"Thank you, Sam, what a lovely breakfast. I do like bacon, is it there under the toast?" Sam reached over, with his own fork, lifted the toast and revealed both bacon and a slice of beef.

"There it all is, if you don't want it all I'll eat it." Sam the romantic.

Maybe Sam could be domesticated, but Tracey had her doubts.

After eating, most of the campers sat drying in the sun, rising from time to time to spread bedding or take a turn in the shower. No one was in a hurry, that would come all too soon.

The humidity was high; Gwen found that the day was already too hot for her as she stood out in the sun looking to the southern sky.

A few minutes later, her helicopter landed. It's first job was to collect Lance, Jane, Harry and Leslie, but where were they? The Professor began to look about, Gwen and Hugh joined him, but of the intended passengers there was not a trace. Questions as to where they might be were evaded with innocent responses by everyone else; it soon became clear that they were in hiding somewhere with the aid of Annie and her helpers.

After a short period Gwen gave up and sent her film crew off to Kununurra instead. She would call for them if she wanted her crew to film the finding of the last two of the Japanese.

As Eric sat talking with the group, Sam and Tracey, breakfast eaten, mugs of tea in hand, walked together down the slope, among the trees with their wet, shiny new green leaves. The sun had quickly dispersed the remaining cloud from the night's storm; it had turned into a clear but decidedly warming up morning, but still suited to young lovers taking an early walk. Sam led Tracey up to that large tree with a big branch that ran out close to the ground. He scooped her up and sat her on it, then stood in front of her with his arms about her waist. What they talked about is their business, all they would tell the others is that they were going to write to and telephone each other regularly, and that Sam was to visit Tracey and her mother as soon as he could.

Shortly after the helicopter departed Annie, surprise, surprise, remembered where her helpers were in the Brolga Springs jungle and brought them back to put them to work.

The two hours passed very quickly, the camp was packed up and the vehicles ready to leave on the trip down the track towards Kununurra. Annie was the only one who was upset at leaving Brolga.

"You two bastards never told me about this place!" she accused Punch and the Professor, "You should have brought me here before. I like this house." The two men knew better than to argue or offer any excuse, Annie was the one who kept their meal plates full; their discomfit amused the rest.

CHAPTER EIGHT.
SEARCHING SOUTH.

T HE SIX 4WD's formed a line as they drove out of the Brolga Springs yard, and began to trek slowly south, over the now newly wet gouged muddy but drying tracks. They were in no hurry, a day or two extra in getting home would not matter, unless it looked like more rain. Sam kept tuning in for the weather; it seemed that the dry spell, except for storms, would continue for a time. Cyclone Hilda was causing widespread torrential rain and great distress as she made her way southward along the Western Australian coast, she was now some thousands of kilometres away from the Kimberley.

Their progress was slow, from time to time they found footprints in the muddy patches on the track, but they had to keep stopping to look for them. The missing men had obviously pressed on with their walk, the footprints that the Professor and Punch found were firm and in a straight line.

By lunchtime that day they reached a deep, clear running creek, with a sandy bottom. There were trees in a shady clump on their side of the creek when they drove up. Sam, who was leading, pulled his wagon into the shade.

"Might have a swim, hey?" he called as the others drove up. Sam was driving with Tracey and Eric as passengers. Chantelle and Natasha, as usual, travelled in the Professor's vehicle, where they had each other to talk to as the Professor drove and concentrated on his own thoughts.

The footprints indicated that the two Japanese had rested for a time at the creek, then walked on.

In no time the men with their stubbies and the girls with most of their clothes still on were in the clear water. Even Natasha. Still the little fussy clean as a whistle miss, she took off only her boots and hat and then in she plunged. The Professor, from his place in a small pool under the shade of a leafy tree, watched them all. He thought Chantelle must have dared Natasha to go in. Bit of a devil in that lively little girl. After twenty minutes of splashing and shouting, they gathered in the shade to eat. More beef, but at least they had bread and jam to go with it now, and plenty of tea. They ate contentedly. After such a good feed, Sam and the mob were ready for a "camp." Swags were chucked down for pillows, and most of them dozed off. The professor wandered away to go for a walk up the creek. He was a little surprised when Chantelle followed and caught him up.

"I come with you, where we goin'?" was her simple statement. The Professor pointed up the creek and kept walking.

It was a pretty place, the rapid flow of clear water over the whitish yellow sand, the new clear pools freshly dug into the creek bed, around the base of the trees that grew in clumps there. The banks were eroded and newly washed, from red to yellow clays and rocks. Along both banks were many trees, from giant paper barks, big ironwoods, boabs in all sizes, bauhinias, they were all there in a carpet of grasses and shrubs. Everything bloomed green and hot, it was very steamy. They came to a pool that swirled around in front of a cluster of trees, just like a spa, they were hot from their walk, Chantelle immediately challenged the Professor;

"I'm going to have another swim." And in they plunged. With the horseplay that followed, their clothes soon came off. The Professor knew, as did Chantelle, that the courtesy of the bush meant they would not be followed or spied on. Chantelle stood on the edge of the pool, facing him in the water. She stood poised and posed, her skin shiny yellow brown in the sun, slightly pendulous round small breasts, long legs, she was just a little skinny, wide thighs with a small thatch of dark hair almost hiding, but not quite, the mysterious slot that halved her mound of Venus. She held out her arms and smiled an invitation.

The Professor rose quickly out of the pool, they laid their clothes in the shade on the sand, and got down together. They kissed and cuddled for a while, and then Chantelle lay back and drew him down to her. It was like starting all over again, out in the daylight without the cover and closeness of the swag in the dark. They moved gently together for a long time, each enjoying their feelings, until with pressure from her hands the now experienced Chantelle told him to hurry. He moved faster, then faster again, when she gasped and whimpered.

"Oh, oh, oh," until she lay still, head against his chest. The Professor was pleased with himself, he had held off under great pressure. He started to move slowly again. Chantelle lifted her head in surprise,

"What are you doing?" she wanted to know. The Professor put his finger across her lips,

"Start moving." he whispered. Soon she did, quicker and faster than before, until she gasped and shouted. It was too much for the Professor, he had wanted to try for three for her, but away he went, shuddering and moaning with pleasure.

Chantelle, when she got her breath back, took both sides of his head in her hands and lifted it up to look at him. The look in her eyes was enough to stir the Professor up again, still together, things started to happen. But it was too hot; they rolled apart reluctantly and plunged back into the pool. They realised that they would be holding the others up, so put their wet gear back on and hurried back to the creek crossing. Chantelle put her arm around him as they walked, looking up,

"I'll never forget you!" she said.

"Now cut that out, remember I've got a missus," he told her sternly.

"Ewye, ewye, that's all right, I remember," was her reply.

It was a concern to the Professor to note that, as they drove south during the next two days, he often caught her shyly looking up sideways at him through half closed eyes. Would she really keep her word and stay away when they got back to Kununurra?

When they returned to the others at the dinnertime camp, following the courtesy of the bush, no one remarked on their extended absence. Chantelle was, however, subjected to continued glares of disapproval from Annie for the rest of the day. Natasha also did not have much to say to her that afternoon. Chantelle shrugged off their condemnation; she was the one basking in the afterglow of love.

They found that Sam already had his vehicle over the creek safely but Bruce had managed to stall. A quick tow and he was out, Punch, the Professor and the Army vehicles soon followed.

The little convoy continued to drive carefully south.

CHAPTER NINE.
THE LAST SURVIVORS.

IT WAS at Tanmurra Creek that they found the two Japanese men. The creek was flowing strongly, with the clear cool water about half a metre deep at the road crossing. The men were very sunburnt, their clothes were torn and tattered, and they were weak with hunger. Their many days of exposure and lack of food left them looking very gaunt, but they were alert and came out from their shelter under a big boab tree to stand waving frantically when the engine noise of the convoy reached them.

Once again it was the story of this ancient land. The Japanese men were starving in the midst of plenty, not knowing what they could eat, and almost dehydrated on the banks of a creek full of sparkling fresh water. But there are things in it, they protested, we might get poisoned. The bushmen had heard enough of this; Sam walked down to the creek, filled his hat and came back up to drink from it with a great display of pleasure. The poor survivors could only look on, surprised.

"The silly buggers don't realise that if there are 'things' in it the water is pure, if it hasn't killed them, it's safe to drink."

Annie decided to have her say. She gathered up a boab nut from under the tree where the survivors had sheltered, took it over to them, cracked it open and began to eat the pith.

"Try this!" she commanded, offering pieces to each. The survivors cautiously nibbled, being too polite to decline. They did not eat much, the pith is quite stringent, and in their partly dehydrated condition they had little saliva to spare. It pleased everyone that they were found in such good shape. Gwen was immediately on the radio to report their success and to call for her helicopter. It was arranged that it would meet the convoy at Tanmurra Bore, where it was proposed the group would camp that night. The Japanese men were given water to sip slowly and were put in the front of Sam's Toyota to travel the short distance to the camp.

Tanmurra Bore is a pleasant camping spot. It is just south of the creek and has a quite large windmill and a big tank with good, fresh water. Surrounded as it is by open grass land, on a slope that has big trees at the top and runs down to the distant creek, it commands a very pleasant view. The Professor, Punch and Sam had all camped there previously, so it was an obvious choice for the camp that night, the first night on their journey from Brolga Springs to Kununurra.

As soon as they arrived, mid afternoon, they got a campfire going, using the firewood that they had gathered since leaving the creek. They made their fire up the slope away from the water trough, so as not to spook the cattle as they came in to drink and began cooking soup and light food for the two Japanese. Until now they had only allowed the men to drink water, aware that after so many days without any food they would have to eat slowly, only eating soft foods or soups, in small quantities. The Professor was puzzled to note that Punch was doing the cooking, with Annie still sitting in his Toyota.

The cooking well in hand, they then broke one of the rules of the bush, most of them went for another swim, this time in the water tank. The normal outlet for the Tanmarra tank, an overflow pipe, regularly blocks up with leaves and algae, so the water runs over the rim. A lot of the normal algae that forms a skin on most tanks then washes over the rim, so the tank has a very clean look inside.

"Jees, what a pity!" exclaimed the Professor, "The overflow is blocked again; we'll have to clean it out!" Getting into the tank to clean the overflow pipe is as good an excuse as any to have a swim. The water was great.

Playing over, they moved further up the slope away from the water trough to set up their swags, leaving it clear for the watering cattle, upwind from the cooking fire already burning with a good hot bed of coals. It was ready for awhile, but except for Punch making soup, no one was cooking. Annie was still sitting sulking in Punch's wagon, the Professor suddenly realising that she had not joined in the swimming.

"What have you done to Annie?" he inquired of Punch.

"Arh, she's got the sulks, spat the dummy, she has, 'cause I want her to stay with me and Sam when we go fishing." He went over to the fire, "Better get something cooking, I suppose."

Sam, Hugh, Gwen, BBC and Bruce had all agreed to stay fishing at the entrance to Tanmarra Creek, where it joined the Ord River, for a few days. This meant that Annie and Judy were also expected to stay with them. The Professor, Chantelle, Natasha and Sergeant Clinton Strong were to go on to Kununurra the next day. Annie was craving the pub life, the lights, the dancing and, she realised, the fuss there might be for the bush rescuers. She could taste the beer already! The Professor went to talk to her.

"You don't want to go fishing, Annie?" No response. "It's a good camp down the Tanmarra, a couple of days there you should get a lot of fish." She looked at him, tears down her cheeks.

"I don't give a bugger about the fish," she said, "I just want a good time! You know that." Indeed I do, thought the Professor, indeed I do.

He sat with her for a time, the sniffling stopped. He pointed to the fire.

"Look at them, that Judy, Chantelle and Punch, trying to cook supper. They need a bit of organising." She sat and watched.

"You missed a good swim," he said, "Remember the one we had in Saddle Creek tank, that very hot day?" The memory of that day brought a smile to her face despite herself.

"This one was just as good, only too many people." What was it with her, she thought, she should hate this man, he would not have her anymore, but he always got her do what he wanted.

"You're a clever bugger, Prof. you think you are so smart." Annie bunched her fist and took a swing at the evading Professor.

"I'll put a leg rope on you when I get back to town, you just watch," she said, her good humour restored, as she got down from the old Landcruiser.

Reaching the fireplace, her directions were soon being issued and followed. Natasha, Judy, BBC and Punch stayed to help. Chantelle soon managed to inconspicuously find her way to where the Professor was talking to Gwen and Hugh.

"What you tell that bitch?" she wanted to know, in a loud whisper.

"I told her to stay here with Punch and Sam," he was happy to truthfully tell her, "and she is." Chantelle was satisfied.

Presently, as they were slowly feeding some soup and little portions of soft food to the Japanese, the helicopter once again found them. It had a doctor on board; he spent time on a careful examination of each man, and approved of the way they were being fed. Gwen and her crew made the most of the recording time this gave them, the news that night had the last rescue to screen, with Gwen's report going out on the helicopter as it took the Japanese men away.

CHAPTER TEN.

THE FRIENDS FROM
THE AIRLINE HIJACKED.

As THE engine noise of the helicopter carrying the last of the Japanese faded away, another was heard. A different helicopter landed. Shock! Asian Pacific had sent it to pick up Eric and Tracey, with firm instructions to also collect Jane, Lance, Harry and Leslie. These four were taken flat footed. There was nowhere to hide on the flat grassy slope at Tanmurra Bore, and with the last stragglers rounded up, they had entirely run out of excuses to stay. Very hasty farewells had to be made; the machine had to leave at once to get back to Kununurra before dark. Confusion reigned, with six leaving the farewells were numerous; baggage was collected, things forgotten and then remembered, it was some time before they were all on board.

A disconcerted Sam found he had little time to make his farewell to Tracey, particularly with the assembled crowd all watching with unfeigned curiosity. He had to be content with the arrangements that they had made the previous day. He was gratified to note that Tracey had tears streaming down her face as she left; he hoped they were for him.

The helicopter had immediately lifted and swung away around the windmill and was gone. A slightly stunned group stood watching emptily, there was a hole in their number that could not be filled. The much reduced group disconsolately turned to the tasks of their camp.

In many ways the two crew members Tracey and Eric had shared very similar experiences in the past two weeks. They had been thrown into desperate situations, been called on for superhuman response and had taken on responsibilities far beyond their training. Both had achieved impossible tasks, at the same time earning the greatest respect from those in their care, and of those with whom they worked. As they had gone from friend to friend, tears flowed, they had a bond of work and hardship shared that would last their entire lives.

There was a general assumption from the group that they would come back, Tracey and Eric had no idea how, but the unspoken word was there. The two crew members had greatly matured over the past week; they now carried an assurance and authority only hinted at before. Woe betide any rude, arrogant passenger who tried to put the new Tracey down in the future, or the Captain who tried to lord it over Eric.

The film crew was pleased to stay and camp another night with the bushie mob, they now regarded themselves as honoury members of Sam's team.

Chantelle was happy again. The thought of both Sam and Annie going fishing pleased her. She had the Professor move his wagon across the slope a bit, away from the scattered large trees and the other cars. Here she set up "their" swag and net. She then went back to help cook, but kept well away from Annie.

All Eric's bottles had been drunk, there was just water and fruit juice to drink before supper, but the now small group was happy and talkative, standing around in the cooking smells.

Natasha came up to the Professor,

"Come boss please show me where to put my swag." She marched away in to the gathering dusk, he following. At his wagon, she turned. "You remember our talk?" she wanted to know.

"Yes."

"Well, what you going to do?"

"How do you mean?" he asked.

"You know what I mean, you going to keep Chantelle for secret girl friend?"

"No."

"Who you having then?"

"Nobody." She turned in exasperation.

"You must have someone?"

"Nobody," he said quietly.

"You want me?" She turned the full benefit of that radiant smile onto him. This time he was prepared, having had time to think matters over.

"Of course I want you! But I can't have you! You forgotten about my missus?"

"You can have her; you can have a girl friend as well, like you did before."

"No more." he said.

She gave a rebutting snort, turned and set about making up her swag. He went slowly back to the fire. As he walked away, Natasha, spreading her blanket, watched the Professor with a knowing expression.

"Some men don't know what they really want!" she exclaimed softly to herself. The Professor may have been a little less complacent with his conversation with Natasha if he had been able to see her look as he walked away.

At the camp fire Gwen reported that she had been talking to the SES on Hugh's radio, the powers that be were making a fuss about Hugh not bringing his Army vehicle back to Kununurra straight away. They were demanding that he and Clinton should then fly out with a new crew to drive the other four vehicles from Yow Springs back to Kununurra. Fishing trips of a week or so were apparently not the go.

"I'm not going to talk to them any more," muttered Hugh, "Gwen can. They can keep their army."

It seemed that he was set to leave the Army, he and Gwen had plans; making love was apparently not the only thing they did in his swag at night. What these plans might be, they kept to themselves.

"The cause of the crash was being blamed on the faulty locking of the cargo hatch door," Gwen said, "They are still investigating everything, it will be months before a report is completed, but it seems that was the problem."

"What are they going to do with the Boeing?" Sam enquired.

"They are to salvage all the parts they can, when the wet is over, and sell the shell to a salvager for its metals. It has to be kept there intact until the investigation is finished." Sam and Punch speculated on the prospects of setting up a tour to the site for the coming tourist season. There was a good deal of banter about how they would go about this as the supper was eaten.

"You'd spend too much time trying to get the young girls into bed," Punch was teased. Annie turned on him.

"Not if I'm there, you better watch it!"

"Wonder if we could use the fuselage as a motel," laughed Punch, "We could call it the Boeing Hilton!" "Or the Boeing Backpackers!"

"I wonder if the smell of the bodies is gone yet?" speculated Punch, "Some were buried in the mud, a bloke would have to dig it all out to make it clean." He had another thought. "Hey, 'B.B'. you reckon that crocodile would come back each night? It might get you yet." The ensuing burst of laughter did not make poor "B.B.C" very happy. He turned to the Professor and Sam;

"You reckon you blokes could spare a tourist each night to feed that big bugger? If the idea was a goer you'd get plenty." The leg pullers and humorists in the group had plenty of ammunition; there was good humour all around.

Sam was in for his share of ribbing, having got away from his crocodile, as was the Professor for not killing it. This led to speculation as to how Lang Harte-Quealey III had got his slash down his leg. Had he tried to cross the creek, also? There were plenty of theories, but no facts.

The absence of Eric and Tracey, (together with that of Lance, Jane, Harry and Leslie) was the cause of sadness in the camp that night. Everyone missed them. However, with plenty of food inside them, not even their normal good natured banter could keep them awake.

Lights went out, the fire died down.

Under their net, Chantelle had some things to say.

"I'm jealousing for that Natasha. What she talk to you about?"

"She asked me if I was keeping you for girl friend." There was a pause.

"Yes?" she asked. The Professor knew when a lie was required; he did not want a full row under his mosquito net.

"I told her yes." Another pause.

"Why she want to know?"

"Because she did not want me to do what Sam did. She likes you."

A naked Chantelle was wrapped around him.

"Well, it was only a little lie." he told himself. If he kept well clear of the streets, as he usually did, especially at night, Chantelle would find it very hard to be his "secret," as she put it.

Chantelle was soon issuing her whispered instructions, weary they might be, but not that tired. The Professor had no time for further thought.

Sam was having a restless night. It was his first night without Tracey. He was not only lonely, he was frustrated as well. Half an hour of tossing and turning, he got up and looked around. It was a brilliantly lit starlight night, he could see around the camp quite clearly.

"I wonder," he thought, "if that Chantelle is still awake. Time I got her back. She don't belong to that Professor." He walked slowly and quietly over to the Professor's mosquito net. As he got close, he became aware of quiet voices.

"Damn," he muttered, if they were both awake he could not sneak her away. As he stood undecided, he became aware of the outline of two pairs of feet under the lower end of the mosquito net. Looking closely, he realised that there was only one thing that the owners of those feet could be doing. A red mist of rage rose up behind his eyes, he lunged forward, reaching for the mosquito net. A sudden realisation of what he was about to do stopped him. There would be an unholy row if he tried to drag Chantelle off, she would set up a great commotion and the whole camp would wake. Everyone in town would know he had a fight with the Professor over a girl; Tracey would get to hear of it. With shaking hand he let the net drop. The two inside were unaware of his presence, they were busy. A self chastened, but self-pitying Sam, returned safely, reluctantly and resentfully to his lonely swag. He would make that Chantelle pay for this.

A decent distance away around the slope Gwen and Hugh were making the most of their short holiday. Hugh was not sure of what he might do for a new job, but he had an idea that his Army life might fit him for the job of park ranger. They both liked this idea; it would allow him to work outdoors, while Gwen could work as a freelance journalist and writer. There then seemed to be a lack of time to discuss the future, other matters required their attention.

CHAPTER ELEVEN.
SOME COME HOME.

I n the morning the town party was soon on their way. Just two vehicles, the Professor's Toyota and Sgt. Clinton Strong in his Landrover. They left behind the three bull catching Toyotas and the Army Landrover driven by Hugh. He had Gwen with him, and had made it known through her that he would wait at Tanmurra Creek until the other Army vehicles arrived there from the coast and then bring it on into Kununurra with them.

The rest of the bushmen, with Annie and Judy, remained to go fishing, moving their camp to the junction of Tanmurra creek where it met the Ord River. The river has high banks here, with fast flowing tidal streams. Sam was sure that they would catch fish.

"It's a good spot, but would be better if we had a boat. Anyone want to go into Kununurra to get one?" He was not surprised when there were no takers.

Both Natasha and Chantelle had chosen to go with the Professor back to town. Chantelle had no wish to be anywhere near Sam if she had a choice. Sam had tried to talk to her, but Chantelle took great care to stay close to the Professor and Natasha. Going fishing, or anywhere else, with Sam, was not on her horizon.

When they reached Eight Mile Mill, Clint Strong was very interested in the track the bushies had followed on their way up, west of the road he and his men had found so difficult. He was chagrined to find that the red soil track used by the bushmen was so much easier than the slog,

slog, slog that the Norforce patrol had endured on their way to the rescue. Heavy sarcasm was not part of the Professor's make up, but Clinton had to endure more than one subtle dig on this subject as they traveled south.

"I wish we had known of this track." Clinton observed to the Professor.

"Well, you had the offer, but the big wigs in the rescue outfit did not want to know. Sam was kicked out of their office, he was firmly told that he was not to go to the crash site, he would only get in the way of you professionals."

Clinton was not amused; he made mental reservations to see that those responsible would get a full serve in his report and that if he was sent on a similar mission in the future bushmen would be his guides.

Well before lunch they reached the big creek half way along the red soil road, it was not running as high as on the way up, it would not be a problem to cross. They parked in the shade of the big boab trees, had a swim, then lunch of corned beef, cold cooked sausages with buttered bread and mugs of tea. They waited until the heat of the day was over, dozing in the shade, then packed up to drive the last leg of the journey to Kununurra.

The red sand track was dry, the last storm had not wet it and by dark, despite the final stretch of the dirt track slowing them up, they had reached the bitumen. They had negotiated the wheel ruts of the bogged tourists and media people who had so recklessly tried to reach the Boeing crash site; it was slow driving, but they did not get bogged. They were further helped by the track knowledge of the Professor, he knew of and regularly used a by pass track through the Tea Cup Springs area, shown to him by 'Scottie the Fisherman' years ago. This track, although they had to be careful, it was also boggy, allowed them to avoid most of the mess made by the other bogged vehicles.

It was therefore a relief for them to arrive at the bitumen and to stop their vehicles on the D4 drain bridge. In haste, prompted by the mosquitoes, they splashed up clean water from the pool on the bridge that is always there in the wet, to clean the mud from their headlights, said their goodbyes to Clint, then both vehicles drove slowly into town.

Chantelle was glad of the dark; she did not want the whole world to see her in the Professor's car. She had him stop at the street before the one in which her mother lived, got out and gave instructions to Natasha as to what was to happen to her blanket roll. She would walk her way home, calling on friends as she did so, to cover her tracks, she said.

The Professor helped Natasha unload the gear at the mother's house, but was caught when he went to get back in to drive away.

"You remember what I said!" was her instruction. She hugged him tight, kissed him firmly. He was surprised again by how much she was trembling, before she released him, turned away and marched into the house. Natasha was experiencing feelings she did not know she had, nor how to handle.

The Professor drove carefully home.

CHAPTER TWELVE.

THE HARTE-QUEALEY CORPORATION.

C UTHBERT LANGFORD HARTE-QUEALEY III did not ever regain what some may have called his senses. He spent his days, in good physical health, sitting trance like, gazing into the distance. On his bad days he would mutter over and over, "There has to be a town, there has to be a town!" He could be raised to frantic action and great excitement if he glimpsed houses or signs of human habitation in the distance, over fields or a valley. His minders had to be careful not to let him see the open countryside. Seeing a picture of a crocodile, or the sight of a stuffed, mounted one sent him into the horrors. He could not bear such a sight; it took hours to calm him down again. This led to some speculation as to the fate of the still missing Steve Roper.

The Corporate minders did not leave him for long in either the Kununurra or Darwin hospitals. It was difficult to determine if their concern was for their boss and his health, or if they were desperately trying to hide his condition from the media and the public. They whisked him away to an exclusive, obscure, expensive clinic in the hills of New York State, where for a time he sank into obscurity.

THE HARTE-QUEALEY CORPORATION, though very wealthy when Lang was able to run it, was soon seen to be on a decline. This process was started by the effects of the penalty clauses in the deal that Lang was trying to reach Sydney to conclude. They were Lang's own clauses; he thought the other party would default. The members of his executive and board tried to hide his condition from the public, some of the more cynical might say he was now better suited to run a multinational, but the word soon spread. The infighting that resulted, put into the terms that are familiar to our bush mates, was that of an organisation running around in ever tightening circles until it disappeared up its own fundamental orifice. Neither the man nor his corporation were missed or regretted.

Helen Anderson, the daily bullied, efficient, now bitter, slightly dowdy private secretary to Lang soon recovered, in Darwin, from her ordeal. As her health improved she spent a lot of time on the telephone, time spent being thoroughly updated on the affairs and happenings of the Harte Quealey Corporation. The information that Helen thus discovered improved her health rapidly.

With her recovery, the dowdiness went, she bought herself smart, stylish clothes, had facials, complete restyle of her hair, manicures, the lot. Under it all she had been a good looking, quite pretty woman, she emerged looking years younger, in fact she was years younger, the stress of her life had made her look older. She moved into a suite in Darwin's best hotel, bank managers came to see her.

She had been very distressed when Lang had argued with Captain Khaw before leading them all away from the crash. Helen found that the two pilots, Captain Anthony Khaw and First Officer Bill Yeo, were still quite ill, but slowly recovering. She visited them daily, then more frequently.

After Gwen had returned from her two weeks holiday with Hugh, Helen made contact with her, to express her gratitude to her for their rescue and the help and sympathy Gwen had given her. A mutual trust and respect for each other developed between these two ladies and they kept in contact by telephone.

With the help of Gwen, Helen discovered that she was a very wealthy woman. Over the years she had built up a portfolio of shares, carefully buying in at the right, legal price the shares of companies that had got the better of Lang in his wheeling and dealing. She rightly concluded that if they could beat him they might be a good investment. She was, mostly, correct. It was not until after the crash that she had arranged to have her position determined, so busy had her boss kept her. She found that the bank account into which her dividends had been paid was a size that frightened her, that she had far more shares than she remembered, and that the number of these shares had increased by conversion of dividends into shares. She was a very wealthy lady, no wonder the dowdiness was swept aside.

After twenty years of very loyal subservience to Langford she emerged, to her daily surprise, as an independent, very attractive lady in her forties. With her complete inside knowledge of the affairs of the Harte-Quealey Corporation she rapidly became a threat to the Corporation men who were desperately trying to save it for themselves.

At Gwen's urging, Helen also took up the matter of her rates of pay, superannuation and accrued leave from the Harte-Quealey Corporation. Given her many years of service, this came to a sizeable sum. It was large enough, given the decline of the company's fortunes, to allow her to negotiate a directorship on the board if she wished in lieu of a cash payment. For the present Helen was content to ponder her decision, a course that subjected her to two types of approaches from the Corporation executives, those who would fawn at her feet, as opposed to those who threatened and abused her.

Helen was generous to the two pilots, especially the Captain, and kept them in Darwin until they were fully recovered. Bill Yeo went back to Singapore, but Tony, as she now called Anthony Khaw, stayed on in Darwin while Helen's newly engaged layers negotiated matters for the two pilots with Asian Pacific. Tony and Helen, by that time, had the appearance, to the outsider, of an established pair.

CHAPTER THIRTEEN.
THE FISHERMEN.

A HAPPY PUNCH, with Annie by his side, had led the fishing party back to Tanmurra Creek after Clinton Strong and the Professor drove off south. After reaching the creek they crossed it to the northern side, after some adventures in doing so. The banks here were steep, yellow slippery mud, the crossing was a loose sandy bottom, with a water flow swift and almost a meter deep, driving across called for skill and, perhaps, some daring.

Once over the creek, they followed the bank for eight or ten kilometres until they reached the junction of Tanmurra with the Ord River. Hugh and Gwen were happy to find that Sam was correct, the banks of both streams here were some meters high, dropping directly into the water, which flowed swiftly in and out with the tide. A good spot for fish, crocodiles and mosquitoes. Despite these discomfits, however, some large shady trees served to make a pleasant and scenic camp site.

Punch may have been happy, but he had to endure a very sullen Annie. She had been too long away from the bright lights, the dancing and singing, the card games under the shady trees by Lily Creek; and the 'gulung", the spring water that restored the spirit and came in brown bottles. Annie's skin was cracking and until she could get back to town Punch would pay the price.

Annie was also not amused that both Natasha and Chantelle had gone with the Professor; she still regarded herself as his. With Judy as her only mate, she also felt that she would be in for more of her share of the cooking and camp duties, with too many males expecting to be catered for.

"Bugger them, they can cook for themselves, I'm going to spend most of my time fishing." And she did; Punch found that in the new camp he was the cook. With everyone fishing, there were soon enough fish to keep him busy. With her sullen bad temper, a turned back in the swag, and her refusal to cook, Punch was not enjoying this fishing holiday, particularly as his camp duties meant he had little time to fish.

In contrast, Gwen and Hugh were in paradise. They were discovering each other, the fishing and the river were just background. Who needed food?

Sam had put up with the fishing trip for just one day. He was not charmed by Punch's basic cooking, he sorely felt the lack of a boat, and fishing from the bank irritated him. And it must be said, a lone swag was not his idea of a holiday. He was also restless to make contact with Tracey. There were no telephones at Tanmurra. There was also the matter of Chantelle. If she would not come back, he would have to find a replacement, a real nuisance so close to the end of the wet.

That night Sam had made his announcement;

"I'm going to town in the morning, to get a boat. This fishing from the bank is the pits; I want a bit of comfort and to be able to move to where the fish are."

Annie was not the only one whose skin was cracking.

"If I can take one of the bullcatching wagons, I'll go with you. Fishing is not for me." Bruce had had his fill of fishing; it was an occupation, as far as he was concerned, that was only tolerable if it was properly lubricated by some good booze.

"I want to go too." Annie's claim was not unexpected, and provoked a night long argument between her and Punch, only resolved the next day when Bruce flatly refused to take her. Bruce well knew that if he agreed to take Annie, Punch would not let the bullcatcher go. Bruce also found that he had to leave Judy behind, as company for Annie. Early in the morning the two vehicles set off, just Sam and Bruce driving them.

The fishing party had then comprised Gwen and Hugh, Harry, BBC and Judy, Punch and a very disgruntled Annie. They set about serious fishing, except for Annie, who sat in the shade and sulked, not even fishing herself and disdainfully refusing to help with the cooking. They were not surprised when Sam, after three days, had failed to return with the promised boat.

Punch was an indifferent cook, Annie's sullen resentment spoiled the camp atmosphere; it was, they decided, time to leave. Annie was then all smiles in anticipation of some partying, Punch was gloomy in the knowledge that he would go back to his "home" block alone.

Gwen and Hugh realised that they had responsibilities to face; it was time to move on. Harry, BBC and Judy were content to follow the lead of Punch and Annie. Despite having enjoyed some excellent fishing, three days later they had all packed up and made their way back to Kununurra.

CHAPTER FOURTEEN.
OF HORSES.

MEANWHILE, NATASHA. She was and is such a private little lady; it was some time before the Professor discovered her surname. Natasha now has her very own horse riding business that she runs very successfully. It caters for the locals, mainly school girls, and for tourists. It is based on a small farm just outside Kununurra. In her neat, tidy brown cowboy hat, check blue shirt, jeans and brown high heel boots, clothes that always seem to look too big for her, Natasha is recognised as a local on her visits to town.

It all came about this way; you remember that Gwen and Hugh were upset at how she cried when she said goodbye to her horses? They did not forget. When Helen found out how much money she had, she asked Gwen if there were people who helped with the rescue she could in her turn help. Gwen told her about Natasha and the horses. They found that Natasha, making plans to return to Queensland, was still on holiday with Chantelle.

This helpful project was just what Helen wanted. A week or two later a helicopter landed at Yow Springs. Gwen, Helen, Hugh and Natasha were on board, so were Gwen's camera crew. Natasha had been enticed to come with them on the pretext that they had to do some more filming at the wreck.

"Would you like to see your horses again?" Would she! The little figure jumped out to walk up the slope. Suddenly she stopped. The Professor was sitting there along the fence line, in the shade, in his old wagon.

"Hurry up," he said, "We've got to get these darned horses of yours moving if we want to get them to Kununurra in the next few days." Natasha gaped at him, turned to see her swag being bundled out of the helicopter, ran back to scramble inside;

"Is what that bastard is telling me true?" She could see by the laughter of the three conspirators that it was, burst into tears, grabbed each one in a small bear hug in turn, scrambled out, grabbed her swag and bag and ran headlong to the Professor, trying to talk to him, to tell him off, to tell him to hurry, and to wave goodbye to the helicopter all at once.

When she got her breath back, and finished admiring the new saddle the Professor said was hers, she rounded on him.

"Boss, there are times when you are a real bastard. But I wouldn't want you any other way. Now hurry up and take me up to see my horses!" The Professor had to sit patiently for some time as Natasha and her three mates renewed their relationship. In due time, riding her best mare, with the other two horses trotting behind, Natasha rode from the yard and headed up the fence line. By night fall they had arrived at Paddy's Bore to camp. Following the trotting horses in his Toyota was a tedious job for the Professor, he was glad to make camp.

There was plenty of fresh grass around the bore and tank for the horses, but the Professor produced hobbles from the depth of his truck to make sure that they did not stray.

Natasha did not like the hobbles, but could see they had no choice. It was still the wet season, all their time would be needed to travel the hundred odd kilometres to Kununurra, they would have no time to look for wandering horses.

While Natasha fed some hay to the horses from the bale on the Professor's truck, he made a fire, produced frypan, steak, potatoes and onions and soon had the air full of that special bush campfire aroma. The tea billy was starting to simmer as he turned the steak. They took their time to eat and to drink their tea; several mugs were each savoured, as they talked over the days events. From time to time, as he related how it had all come about, the Professor found that he was a bastard. This did not unduly disturb him; the word in the bush is used more for affection than abuse. Natasha had a worry;

"Boss, I thought these horses belonged to the station?"

"Well, yes, they did, but when Gwen and Helen fluttered their eyes at the station manager, and told him what you had done with them, what else could he do but give them to you?" The Professor did not add that the horses were regarded by the station as pensioners, anyway, too old for further hard work.

As the camp fire died away, they prepared their swags, one each side of the fire. As was his custom, the Professor rigged up his mosquito net, using a steel fence post he carried in his truck for this purpose for one end and the side of his Toyota at the head of the swag. Natasha found that she also had a mosquito net, wrapped in her swag, but she was at a loss how to put it up. For a brief moment she sat looking at how the Professor had his arranged. She made up her mind and walked around the fire.

"Boss, we don't need two nets, I can fit my little swag in with yours." This was a statement, not a question. The Professor could only watch as her swag was swiftly placed under his net. He said nothing as he stripped down to his pyjamas, just a pair of black stubby shorts. Aware as he was of Natasha's feelings for him, the Professor wondered what the night might bring. She had already disappeared under the net, as was her custom, fully clothed. The intense dark of the tropical, cloudy night moved in as the fire flickered out.

What may have transpired under that net that night and the nights that followed on the leisurely journey to Kununurra is known only to the Professor and Natasha. The gentleman in the Professor totally forbids him to discuss any intimate relationship he may or may not have had with any lady.

Natasha, being the private person that she is, certainly will not speak of such things. Suffice it to say that whenever in the future Natasha heard the names of Paddy's Bore or Tanmurra her brown countenance suffused with red, a most unusual occurrence, quite out of character. To all appearances it was a very close and happily related pair of friends who in due time arrived back in Kununurra.

The Professor had arranged for the horses to be temporarily minded on one of the small farms on the Weaber Plains Road until the site for Natasha's riding school was chosen and leased. Helen and Gwen were organising this and having a great time. Natasha knew just exactly what she wanted, it was not too elaborate or expensive and she was so appreciative of all they were doing for her. Helen had the Professor choose the land for Natasha, and had him on hand for advice and work. The Professor knew who to see, who was best for putting up the buildings; he had water tanks and pumps installed, supervised the building of sheds and a small two roomed house with verandas all around for Natasha to live in. A bush type kitchen on one veranda completed the house. He also made arrangements for Helen to buy some new, younger horses to increase her team, but, good as they were, Natasha never did lose her special affection for her three veterans from Attack Bore.

Unknown to the Professor and Natasha, Helen had arranged the subdivision and purchase of the land used by Natasha, and planned to gift it to her at a suitable time.

Now that it is all in place and functioning under Natasha's firm hand, the Professor can often be seen sitting on a rail of the horse yard watching the antics of the tourists. Natasha is kind and gentle to her horses, and rough as bags on her customers and the tourists, something they seem to like.

This project for Natasha was the first joint work done by Helen and Gwen. They enjoyed working together, and it was not long before the idea of Gwen coming to work for Helen occurred to both of them. But first, the affairs of the Harte-Quealey Corporation had to be dealt with.

CHAPTER FIFTEEN.
MORE CORPORATE BUSINESS.

DESPITE THE frantic efforts of the directors, the affairs of the Harte-Quealey Corporation continued to unravel. The process was accelerated by the "in house" squabbling of the remaining executives. Helen was continually surprised by the jealousies and resentments that surfaced. As these squabbles emerged the directors found it convenient to hold their meeting in Sydney, as Gwen, who was their problem, flatly refused to meet them in New York. After attending some of these fruitless meetings of the remaining board Helen confided in Gwen;

"I feel rather uncomfortable facing that board on my own, Gwen, could you please come with me?"

"I certainly will." agreed Gwen promptly and a few days later they entered the meeting together. This provoked a fuss, but in the end Gwen was allowed to sit in as an adviser.

The Harte Quealey Corporation had a long history, having been established as part of the family's corporate structure in the time of Langford's father. On this gentleman's death, Lang had received it as part of his family inheritance, having for many years been in charge of this section of the family affairs.

The shareholding position of the company was rather obscure. It was not a public company, but it had in the past awarded to it's employees parcels of shares as bonuses or incentives. As one of the longest term existing employees Helen had participated in all these issues; in fact it appeared that if at any time she had been owed money, perhaps in lieu of leave, it had been convenient for Lang Harte-Quealey to pay her off in this manner, thus saving cash.

To the anguish of the other directors, they discovered that Helen was a major shareholder in the Corporation, her holding almost as large as Lang's. Helen only needed to have the support of one other of the directors to control the company. The remaining directors combined could not then outvote her if she had that support or if she were to hold the proxy votes of Lang's shares.

With the moral support of Gwen, Helen set about gaining control of the affairs of the Corporation. A long period of horse trading and outright hostility began.

It was pointed out to her by Gwen that if Helen could contact the former and existing employees of the Corporation, she might be able to buy some of their shares until she had enough to completely control the company in her own right. Helen grasped the importance of this move and at once set up an office of her own in Darwin in the building where her newly engaged solicitors had their offices, to bring this about.

With some diffidence, not wishing to appear too patronising, Helen offered Gwen the job of running this office and tracking down the shareholders. Gwen was flattered; she appreciated the skills with which her journalistic work had equipped her and the contacts she had, and promptly set about using these assets.

It soon became apparent that many of these shareholders were aware of the incapacity of Lang and thus the failing prospects of the Corporation, with what appeared to be the incompetence of the remaining directors. They realised that selling their shares at this time for what seemed to be a good offer from Gwen made sense, so they quickly made a deal. Using the fears of some as to the future value of the shares Gwen was able to secure some parcels at bargain prices.

Fighting amongst themselves, travelling to and from Sydney and New York, holding many inconclusive meetings, the other directors were totally unaware of what Helen was organising until it was too late.

Helen was very pleased with Gwen's efforts.

"Gwen, I don't know how you did it, but your splendid work has helped me enormously. I want you to accept the last parcel of shares that are on offer to us as yours."

Gwen was flabbergasted.

"No, Helen, I can't accept them, you pay me very well for what I do!" she exclaimed.

"Nonsense, my dear, unless you are a shareholder I can't really appoint you a director to vote for me, so you must take them."

The day came when Helen determined she had the numbers. She called a meeting to be held in Sydney, took Gwen, Tony and also Hugh along, and had her showdown. She could outvote them all, in her own right, except for the vote of the share holding of Lang. These shares were being held in escrow, pending determination as to the mental condition of Lang, and thus were not available for voting purposes at short notice, by proxy or otherwise. So Helen could call all the shots, at this meeting, for the time being.

The first heads to roll were those of the so overbearing Corporation men who had totally ignored her when Helen and her two fellow workers were found at Brolga Springs. They had been so eager to get the credit for finding and rescuing Lang that they not only ignored these distressed survivors, except for trying to keep Helen away from Gwen's microphone, they had also refused to let the Corporation helicopter fly them out until forced to do so.

"You were totally selfish pigs when you met us at Brolga Springs," Helen stated, "all you cared about was to get the credit for finding Lang for yourselves. You also displayed little sympathy for any others while you searched for Lang, and tried to bully Hugh and his men. You will resign as directors of this company today, now, at this meeting, or we will vote you out anyway. You will also offer all your shares to me at a price to be agreed, or we will vote as directors to have your shares bought back by the company at an average price."

The two made a lot of empty threats and bluster, but out they went.

Helen then turned her attention to the Director who had displayed such an overbearing manner when he arrived after they had found Lang. He was taken aback to find that no matter what he did or said, he was outvoted; he was totally frightened by the severity and determination displayed by Helen, their new chairman, the previously quiet and efficient private secretary.

Up against the wall, thoroughly cowed by her ferocity, this gentleman hastily agreed to Helen's terms. He was to sell to her half his shares, and to brief her, Gwen and Hugh on all the current activities of the Corporation. If he did so, he could remain as a director, on what were, Helen suggested to him, under the circumstances, generous directors fees.

Helen came away from this meeting in complete control of the Corporation, except for the obscure future ownership of the shares held in escrow for Lang.

Gwen was not aware before hand that Hugh was to be briefed on the affairs of the Corporation. After the meeting concluded she turned to Helen for an explanation. Helen was developing a liking for springing surprises on her friends. Hugh and Gwen had yet to be told of the job she had for Hugh.

Gwen had, for some time, been surprised at Helen's preoccupation with the affairs of the Harte-Quealey Corporation. At the briefing from the Directors that followed the crucial meeting, Gwen suddenly realised that with her years of working for the Corporation Helen knew more about how it worked, how to set up the deals that it brokered, than anyone else except, possibly, for Lang himself.

In her dealings with the directors and now ex-directors Helen had displayed a ruthlessness and determination that had surprised them all. All her years of submission to the workplace demands of Lang had, it seemed, equipped her well for the future.

It was evident that the directors had been under the total control of Lang, he had directed and organised their every move. None of them were capable of running the Corporation, either alone or jointly

In pursuit of her aims, and still unknown to her fellow active directors, Helen had her team of solicitors and agents continuing in their efforts to quietly locate the few remaining private shareholders in the Corporation, in most cases successfully arranging deals to buy their shares. The careful and quiet accumulation of these shares resulted in Helen being the new boss of the Harte-Quealey Corporation, in her own right, no longer having to depend on any other director or the proxy of Lang's shares. In fact, her shareholding was now such that she would still be in total control even if the shares held by Lang were released and sold off to others. Of course, if these shares were released, Helen would be a serious buyer for them.

While these share purchases did make a dent in her bank account balances, Helen was happy to note that the bargain prices that Gwen at times achieved for her, and the subsequent total value of her now large parcel of Corporation shares and the other assets of the Corporation, gave her substantial financial clout.

With the appointment of Gwen as a director, Helen had complete control of all meetings. She then set about entering into contracts just as Lang had done, to resurrect the income basis of the Corporation. Gwen, Hugh and Tony were fascinated at the skill and tactics that she used in pursuit of these aims. Unwittingly, Lang had taught her well.

The name Harte-Quealey Corporation had no appeal any longer for Helen, she set the wheels in motion to have it changed to Darwin Brokering Services Corporation.

When a new parcel of shares came on offer, Helen sprang another of her surprises.

"Tony, I want you to have these shares, so you can also be a director. I will need your support at future meetings in New York."

CHAPTER SIXTEEN.
CAPTAIN TONY.

WORKING STEADILY away in her Darwin office Gwen received a message from a pilot in Hong Kong asking if Helen was now in charge of The Harte-Quealey Corporation and if so what was he to do with their executive jet and could he please have some pay? When advised of this massage, Helen exclaimed;

"The Lear in Hong Kong! With all the fuss with the directors, I totally forgot about it. If it had not broken down in Hong Kong we would not have all been on the Boeing. That plane has something to answer for; I'll put it to good use!"

"Gwen, please contact this poor pilot, see if the jet has been repaired and is airworthy and arrange for his proper pay."

Greatly intrigued, Gwen did so. She soon found that the aircraft had been repaired and was in an airworthy condition, but that the repairs had not been paid for. She also discovered that some of the directors had been trying to get the use of the aircraft, but had been too mean to pay the substantial repair bill. They had imagined that they would be able to vote for this expense to be paid by the Corporation, as it indeed now was, but too late for them to seize it.

The pilot, it transpired, was the original second officer, the skipper having given up and found another job. Helen remembered him, a decent young fellow by the name of Terry Wall.

Helen was able to call him up.

"Terry, this is Helen Anderson, you may remember me, I was private secretary to Lang?"

"Yes ma-am, I do remember you, are you my new boss now?"

"I expect you could say that, Terry. First, I want to thank you for staying with our jet, and getting it all organised. I have looked at the records; you are qualified as a skipper, so we will pay you at that rate for your time since you were stranded in Hong Kong." A grateful Terry could only, in his surprise, stammer;

"Thank you, ma-am, I did not expect such generous treatment." Terry was overcome; his dealings in the past month with the other directors had left him quite apprehensive as to his fate. He had, in fact, started to look for another job. Helen continued.

"Also, Terry, I will ask you to meet a new director of our company, Anthony Khaw, who was the skipper of the Boeing that we were all in when it crash landed. He has, he tells me, flown Lear Jets, but some time ago, so he will need updating." A shaky response.

"Yes, ma-am."

"I would like it if you and Anthony, you may call him Tony when you get to know him, can bring the jet to Darwin. You will probably be based in Darwin, but we will go into all that when you get here."

"Yes, ma-am." Helen was confident that she had won a new, loyal employee, indeed, even a new friend.

Later that day she spoke to Tony, briefing him fully as to what the position was with the Lear Jet, concluding;

"I would like you to fly to Hong Kong, meet Terry, and bring the jet back here. I have promoted him to Chief Pilot, as you will also be, when your conversions are confirmed. This should not be any problem, as you will not fly the jet often. We will probably have to find a young pilot to be First Officer when you are not flying with Terry." A surprised Tony agreed, and was soon in the air on the way to Hong Kong.

Helen was very pleased with recovering the jet. It would enable her to move swiftly to and from Darwin, Sydney and New York, with the special advantage of having Tony, not only as pilot, but in his role of director, and companion, with her.

Her satisfaction was, however, short lived. Lang had, apparently, divorced a previous wife. She had been receiving a generous monthly settlement payment, but this had suddenly ceased, the trustees who held

Lang's assets in escrow determined that he was no longer obliged to meet this payment, as he was not now receiving any income, directors fees and dividends having for the time being ceased. This, of course, enraged her, and she began a legal action to take ownership and control of Lang's shares, and the Corporation if she could. Helen, of course, decided to contest this, and put Gwen in charge of any appropriate action.

Gwen found she had a serious problem, not only did the disgruntled wife want all Lang's shares, she wanted a directorship as well, and to chair the board. In this she was being encouraged by the two dismissed, disgruntled former directors.

CHAPTER SEVENTEEN.
TRACEY'S COURTSHIP.

S AM QUICKLY abandoned his pretence that his return to Kununurra was to find a boat. As soon as he arrived home, he was on the telephone to Singapore. Tracey, he found, was at home with her mother, on two weeks leave, before she had to return to duty.

"Can I come for a visit?" There followed a muffled and hasty consultation between Tracey and her mother.

"Yes." He was assured, "You can come, but you will have to stay at a hotel, we do not have enough room for you in our apartment." This was no deterrent to Sam, within minutes he had a flight booked to get him to Singapore in two days time. Tracey was to meet him at the Changi Airport.

On his arrival, to Sam's intense irritation, he found that Tracey was not alone, mother was also there. He found that, in the next few days, everywhere that they went, mother was constantly accompanying her daughter, a situation that Sam had to accept as permanent. Sam's time with Tracey was also restricted by her work schedule.

Sam was driven to distraction by this. No matter how he contrived and planned, mother was one step in front. Despite this, he found that she was a very nice person; she just kept a very close eye on Tracey. Mrs. Leong was determined that Tracey was not going to be used by a man as she had been. Her daughter was not going to be allowed to give herself to a man who might then leave her, pregnant and alone, as her RAAF pilot, Tracey's father, had done.

Even at home, sitting with Tracey in front of the television, Sam could not achieve anything. A short time alone, some serious petting under way, when, at the door;

"I've just made a new cup of tea, do you two want some?" A groan from Sam, an acceptance from Tracey as she hastily untangled herself.

"Oh, God, please get rid of that woman!"

"What did you say, Sam?" Tracey was amused, Sam tortured.

All too swiftly his holiday ended, Tracey, complete with mother, saw Sam off on his flight home. As he sat and dozed on his way to Darwin, Sam realised that Tracey was out of his reach until a wedding had been celebrated.

On his return to Kununurra, Sam called Tracey every day that she was off duty at home, creating a telephone bill that made him wince when it came. The courtship was long and greatly wearying on Sam's patience. Two more trips to Singapore did no more than deplete Sam's bank balance.

His misery was also compounded by his lack of a lady to replace Chantelle. He was well aware that any such activity would be made known to Tracey, she now had many loyal friends among the Kununurra "bushies."

Part of his problem was to also get the approval of mother Leong. It was to be many months before her mother was convinced that Sam was sincere in his courting. Eventually she agreed to a Kununurra wedding for the pair, on the condition that she also was to live there when Tracey was married. If Sam thought these arrangements were to end his strife, he underestimated the will of mother Leong. The wedding preparations and planning were almost, he found, as wearying as his courtship.

Contractors such as Sam have to keep working, no work, no money, and Sam was spending his fast. He was forced to take on some fencing, assemble a crew and try and supervise them with sporadic visits from town. Not a good idea. Sam found he had to spend his mornings with his fence crew, late afternoons organising builders etc. in town, then a night drive back for a couple of hours sleep in the camp before, in the dawn, leading the fencers in their days work. It was not a good time to upset him, as some of his fencers found.

In addition to all the wedding arrangements, Sam found that he had to organise the building of the granny flat for Tracey's mother, and to refurbish his own house to a standard that would suit Tracey. The furnishings that were adequate for Chantelle had to be replaced, walls were painted and curtains fitted to windows. There was much consultation by telephone and on Sam's chaste, virginal visits to Singapore.

CHAPTER EIGHTEEN.
THE CIVIC RECEPTION.

A GRATEFUL ASIAN Pacific Airlines arranged for the Shire in Kununurra to hold a civic reception for the rescuers. This proved to be very difficult for the Shire as some of the bushies were very reticent to be so regailed. They were never all available in the town at the same time. In desperation the Shire President decreed, after two months had elapsed, in the realisation that there was little chance of all being in the one place, that the reception should be held forthwith.

The purpose of the reception was to express the thanks of the Airline to the locals, the "bushies" and the Norforce men, for their part in the rescue of the distressed passengers.

The Airline was well aware and appreciative of the danger, discomfit and the effort that these volunteers endured in their selfless rescue and support actions. The function was also to be used as a venue for the announcement of coming events; such as the anticipated weddings of Nugget and Adelaide, Lance Park and Jane Burrows, perhaps Harry Green and Leslie Roberts, together with, surprise, surprise, that of Tracey and Sam. This was anticipated to be a big event in the early future.

The reception, though small, was a happy event. The Shire Councillors were all present, the Colonel and his SES people, a small clutch of Asian Pacific Airlines executives, Helen, with Tony, Gwen and Hugh from the new Darwin Brokering Services Corporation (formerly Harte-Quealey Corporation), plus the soldiers from Norforce.

The Professor was present with Mrs. Professor, accompanied by Natasha. The Professor was pleased that Chantelle was wise enough to accept the situation and that she did not put any further claim on him other than that of a casual friend. Natasha watched them all very carefully.

Looking around, the Professor and Sam were disappointed to note that the airline had not thought it proper to ensure that First Officer William Yeo, Second Officer Eric Peng and, of most importance to Sam, Senior Cabin Attendant Tracey Leong were present. This omission was also carefully noted by Helen.

Sam was despondent until the announcement that a grateful Asian Pacific Airlines had decided to award the bushmen and their ladies a pass for two trips a year for five years from Australia to any of the cities in Asia that they served. This was just what he needed, two more trips off to Singapore in the next few months to visit Tracey.

The Shire President then spoke;

"Ladies and gentlemen, on behalf of the Shire and the State Government I have the good fortune and great pleasure to tell you of a special award that has been made to all those civilians who contributed so well to the rescue operation. I will call your names so that you may come forward and accept your certificates and the special medal."

Some of the recipients were not present; their awards were set aside for a future occasion. At the end of the presentations, with sudden realisation, Sam, Punch and the Professor spoke in unison;

"What about Natasha? She deserves an award also!"

"Indeed she does," the President agreed, "and this has been arranged. Natasha, please come forward and accept your special award for bravery and exceptional devotion to duty." A blushing and flustered Natasha accepted her award to great applause, but was so overcome that all she could do was bow to the President, turn to her supporters and splutter;

"Thank you, thank you." before retreating in haste.

Gwen was able to announce that, despite a lot of bureaucratic obstruction and bother, little "Mudlark" was still being fostered by Nugget and Adelaide, with the help of Helen and her Corporation. Further, that to keep the bureaucrats at bay, Adelaide and Nugget had advanced their wedding plans, to be married as soon as possible. And, of most interest to the "bushies", that their plans were to celebrate their wedding with all their "crash" friends present in Kununurra. This announcement provoked an enthusiastic round of genuine applause.

Annie, true to form and despite Punch's efforts, made full use of the hospitality of the reception, drinking and dancing in complete enjoyment. She was soon way past remembering anything. Punch, after the first few drinks was almost as abandoned as Annie, although his enjoyment was tempered by the need to keep an eye on her, making sure, if he could, that her favours were kept for him and not shared around. They awoke next morning, in someone's camp, very late, down by the creek in the scrub, with very little idea of the good time that they had presumably enjoyed, but with grinding hangovers to mark this enjoyment.

It was a few days before they discovered about the airline passes. Annie, being the sociable lady that she is, was very pleased and made immediate plans to make full use of her privilege, visiting Tracey in Singapore and through her making new friends for the parties and dances she loved. Punch was not impressed; he made no use of his at all. Some of the other bushies made use of their pass from time to time.

The Professor was to use his full entitlement, being very careful to ensure that his journeys were at different times to Annie's. There were many places that he had read of in Asia that he wanted to see for himself.

Annie rated the reception as a top event; Punch was sick for days later and viewed it in a far different light.

CHAPTER NINETEEN.
TRACEY'S WEDDING.

I T DID not start out to be a big affair, but as the word spread, Sam found that he was to host a full scale social event. The bushmen and their ladies all had to be invited, Sam's fencing and station mates could not be left out, Gwen, Helen, Hugh and Tony Khaw were compulsory and presently the names of "Nugget", Adelaide and Kimberley were added to the lists. Then there was Lance Park, Jan Burrows, Leslie Roberts and Harry Green. These four took advantage of their being in Kununurra to arrange for their own Kununurra weddings later that year. Everyone involved was filled with delighted anticipation of a great event, all except Sam's bank account balance, which took a proper belting.

Sam examined his statement at length and with pain, what with the costs of his visits when in Singapore, refurbishing his house and now this wedding thing, Tracey was becoming an expensive bride. Sam wisely kept this pain to himself, well aware of the derision that would come his way from the "bushies" if they found out. They would, without tact, and with cruel, basic ribaldry, have pointed out to Sam that Chantelle and her predecessors had cost him very little, that at last he was having to pay for his companion.

Some weeks before the big day, Tracey left her job with the airline, and arrived with her mother to stay at a Kununurra hotel. To his disgust Sam found that he was not allowed access to their hotel room unless mother Leong was present, and that the two went together on shopping trips, inspections of the house and granny flat and at all times when Sam showed them the wonders of the Kimberley. Conjugal happiness was clearly not available until the knot was tied.

"Tracey" suggested Sam, "you could save some money if you and your mother were to stay in my house until the wedding."

"Sorry, Sam, but mother would not feel comfortable there." Subject closed; no further discussion.

In due time the great day arrived. The Kununurra church was filled to overflowing; this was one event that the locals were not going to miss. A very nervous and immaculately suited Sam waited in front of the altar, with best man Punch, supported by Eric Peng. (The Airline had flown some of their people to Kununurra for the wedding, aware of the poor reaction to their not doing so for the Civic Reception.) Also awaiting the bride was matron of honour Annie and bridesmaids Fong Susan and, of course, Natasha.

Susan, you will recall, was the brave little hostess with the broken arm who insisted on doing her full share of caring for the passengers after the crash. Tracey could not overlook her.

A radiant and very beautiful Tracey, poised, happy and aware of the importance of the occasion, advanced down the aisle on the arm of a proud and smiling Professor, who nodded greetings to all but was careful to avoid the eyes of Chantelle. Try as he would, he could not evade the beaming smile of Natasha as the bridal party turned to welcome the bride. Having deposited Tracey into the care of her bridegroom and answering the inquiry of the priest with a firm;

"I do!" the Professor retired to the back of the church, where "Mrs. Professor" was hard pressed to keep him a seat. The crowd overflowed down the church steps and out into the street. After the signing of the register and wedding papers, the priest led them forth to announce;

"Ladies and gentlemen, I introduce you to Mr. and Mrs. Samuel Wrightson" to enthusiastic applause.

When the newlyweds emerged from the church there was some difficulty clearing access for the official cars as the bridal party were eventually whisked away for the photo session. Most of the congregation chose to walk to the Civic Centre for the reception. Here tables were arranged in more than half of the large hall, with places set and names on cards for all the invited guests. Finding their allotted seats took some time, hampered as the search was by those who were not official guests but were hopeful.

The Professor found he had a problem. As the man who gave away the bride he was allocated a seat at the top table, but found that his own wife was not seated with him. When the bridal group returned from the photo session he voiced his concern.

"Sam, I can't sit at the top table without my wife. Where can we sit together?

Hurried rearrangements were made, two seats at the next table down were arranged, where the Professor could be seated with his lady, yet be available for a speech when called upon.

Those who did not find a seat were content to sit on the spectator dais along the side of the hall or to sit in the café seats in the foyer. Once the bridal party were seated relative quiet was restored.

Toasts were proposed and drunk and many things were said in the speeches that caused embarrassment for Sam, to the delight of all. He was glad when the compulsory bridal waltz and the formalities were all over. They watched the dancers, led by an exuberant Annie, for a time, then left to change into their travelling clothes. The location for the honeymoon was, of course, a secret, but most supposed, incorrectly, that Lake Argyle resort would be chosen. Before they could be followed the newly weds drove around for a time through the Kununurra back streets and then away on the road to Wyndham.

"That will trick them; let the smart buggers try to find us now." Sam exclaimed to his new bride, alone with her at last.

"Where are we to stay tonight?" enquired Tracey.

"At the Wyndham hotel, they have prepared a special room for us, no one will expect us to be there. In two days time, when, I hope, they have given up trying to find us we are booked to move out to El Questro."

"Won't they be able to find us by our bookings?" Tracey wanted to know.

"For the last few hours you have been the new Mrs. Wrightson, my lovely new wife, but for the next week you will be Mrs. Right in the hotel registers," explained a complacent Sam.

Tracey thought this over for a time.

"What about this car, if we use it or park it anywhere they might find us?"

"Don't worry, early in the morning the car hire company will bring us another, differently coloured car and take this one away. This car will be seen in Kununurra, let them work that out."

Their arrival at the Wyndham Hotel was anticipated, they were quietly installed in that hotel's best room, and left alone with the customary bottle of champagne.

That night Sam was to discover, to his astonishment and chagrin, that there was a lot more to love making than his customary "slam, bam, thank you ma-am" routine of his past. Tracey was fortunate that her mother had gained much more than just a daughter from her RAAF pilot love affair. Her young man had been a kind, experienced lover, aware of how to please his partner. Mother Leong, once the wedding was a definite decision, had spent many hours of instruction with an embarrassed Tracey on the rites of love making.

San found his night was long, he had much to learn, his impatience was worn down by a resolute Tracey, before dawn all was well. In future nights Sam found that his lessons, properly learnt, were rewarded. He found it difficult and unrewarding to reflect on his past love making.

CHAPTER TWENTY.

DARWIN BROKERING SERVICES CORPORATION.

TRUE TO her wishes Helen took Tony and Gwen to New York and between them they negotiated all the obstacles to complete the changing of the name of the Harte-Quealey Corporation to Darwin Brokering Services Corporation. It was their intention to maintain the now principal office of the corporation under Gwen's control in Darwin, with offices in Sydney and New York.

Gwen found that she was becoming more and more involved in the day to day running of the affairs of the renewed Corporation, leaving Helen free to devote her time to their core business, brokering. The disruption to the Corporation brought about by Lang's illness and the board changes had drastically reduced it's income, it took all her accumulated knowledge and skill for Helen to get it back onto a profitable income basis.

Hugh had for some time been employed by the Corporation, for the most part assisting Gwen. Helen decided, on their return from New York, to give him a definite job.

"Hugh, I would like you to become more involved in financing and brokering more deals in the IT industry. Would you like to become our senior advisor in this field?" A flustered Hugh responded;

"I don't know much about the stuff, how could I do such a job?"

"Well, there are ways that you could learn some of the basics, and with your people management skills I am sure that you could soon suss out the genuine people from the dreamers and scoundrels."

So Hugh found himself doing computer courses and studies, and dealing with many in the industry, finding to his surprise that he enjoyed, in due time, his new job, and was able to guide Gwen to many successful, suitable deals. He also was able to give the push to many that were not viable, or perhaps deliberately dishonest.

To her irritation, Gwen had to spend considerable time in New York countering the demands of the divorced wife. Gwen found that the lady was quite vindictive and unreasonable, no doubt influenced by the two sacked directors providing her with a highly coloured version of Helen's assumption of control of the Corporation. The lady was under the impression that she was automatically entitled to Lang's shares. It was not until Gwen was able to impress upon her that, if she was not more reasonable, she might end up with nothing but a large legal bill that negotiations resumed in a more rational atmosphere.

Gwen used her skills to finally arrange for some of Lang's shares and the balance of his available money to be allocated to the lady, sufficient to pay her a living allowance. The former wife was also given title to the house used by Lang and herself as a country retreat, and where she was now living, at Parksville, a small town in the foothills of the Catskill Mountains, in the upper regions of New York State.

It was here, where Gwen was able to visit Mrs.Harte-Quealey and to establish a reasonable relationship with her, that Gwen was able to reach a settlement. The realisation that she was to be given the house where she lived, with income, clinched the deal, and removed any hostility. Gwen was given to understand that a visit by Helen, who was, of course, known to Mrs. Harte-Quealey, would be welcomed.

The rest of the shares were sold to Helen, with the funds raised from this sale used to establish a trust to keep Lang in a suitable home for mental invalids. This facility was located at Wells, a small town in the Adirondack Mountains area, upstate New York. The wooded grounds and lush green lawns here bore no resemblance to the harsh sea shore landscape of the North Kimberley where he had been found; the landscape that disturbed him so much. Here he spent his days in a docile condition, sitting motionless for long periods and in co-operation with the nursing staff. The dynamic tycoon seemed to have entirely disappeared. The medical reports on Lang's condition made it apparent to all that it was unlikely that he would ever recover, his state, the specialists concluded, being the result of some trauma of catastrophic proportions. The nature of this event was not known to them, and provided a basis for their unsuccessful research for many years

CHAPTER TWENTYONE.
NATASHA'S DAUGHTER.

I<small>T WAS</small> some months after Tracey's wedding that the regular riders and customers at Natasha's little riding school noticed that their instructor seemed to be putting on weight. Any such suggestion was promptly denied by Natasha, but it became obvious that her jeans and checked shirt were no longer a loose fit.

On her visits to the town to grocery shop and collect mail, Natasha was in the habit of visiting Tracey to enjoy with her a gossip and a cup of tea. Natasha was a little put out when Tracey joined the band of those who accused her of gaining weight.

Tracey gave her a playful poke in the stomach and was surprised to find how hard it was. Natasha clearly resented her familiarity.

"Now calm down, Natasha, if you are not putting on weight, what are you doing?"

Natasha did not respond. Tracey decided that she could not let the matter drop.

"Come 'Tashie'," she coaxed, "Off with your shirt and let's have a look at that tummy of yours." A very reluctant Natasha let her shirt be removed, to reveal that she could no longer fasten the top buttons of her jeans.

"Well, well, 'Tashie, what have we here!" exclaimed Tracey. "It looks like you have a baby on the way. Do you?"

Natasha could only stammer;

"I don't know."

"Have you been to the hospital for a check up?"

"No."

Tracey took over.

"We'll ring for an appointment today, I'll take you around to the hospital, and we will find out all about it."

Later that afternoon it was all known to Natasha and Tracey. Natasha was intensely embarrassed to have to answer questions on her periods, sexual relations and other personal details. She was found to be pregnant, to probably be in her fifth month and to be very healthy.

Tracey took her back to have another cup of tea and to talk things over.

"You will have to take proper care of yourself, 'Tashie', and eat and drink the proper foods. Moving large hay bales, saddling horses and mucking out stables might be too much for you soon. Is there anyone who can do some of these things for you?"

Natasha looked a little startled; these were complications that she had not expected.

"Perhaps one of the older riders might like to come and work for you?" suggested Tracey. Natasha considered this idea for a time.

"I would have to pay such a worker. I have some money in the bank, but how much should I pay, and how do I go about this?"

Tracey at once came to her rescue.

"You find your worker and how much pay he/she would expect, and I'll take it from there. I can arrange your tax and pay records, and do all that for you."

Tracey had been quietly speculating to herself as to who the prospective father might be. Natasha had not given her the slightest indication of this. She decided to try a question or two to try and find out.

"Is there anyone else who might be able to help with the heavy work?" she innocently enquired. Natasha's response was an abrupt and adamant;

"No!"

Tracey decided that she had better let this matter alone. Privately, she had her own ideas, the Professor was often to be seen at the riding school, but as to their relationship Tracey was in the dark. The Professor did not appear to have any particular task, but if any difficulty arose he rapidly responded for any call for help made by Natasha. Otherwise he seemed to be just an interested onlooker.

So, when Natasha's time duly arrived and she was delivered to the hospital by the ever attentive Tracey, the affairs of the riding school were in safe hands, the hired worker a capably assistant, Tracey doing the accounts, all under the benevolent eye of the Professor.

Tracey Helen was duly born, without complications, despite her small size Natasha was able to give birth naturally, after a few hours delay. Many of the riding school regulars paid hospital visits to their popular teacher; her room was soon filled with flowers and presents. Natasha appeared to be astonished to find that she was indeed a mother, and truly grateful for all the good wishes and attention.

When the time came for her to go home, Natasha was collected from the hospital by Tracey. They were both surprised to find that a baby cot, pram and stroller had mysteriously been delivered the day before, at whose initiative, this seemed to be a mystery.

Tracey Helen was a good, contented, happy little brown skinned baby, and Natasha was happy to find that she could breast feed her. The customers at the riding school were charmed and delighted at the picture of mother and daughter at feeding time, settled on the house veranda where Natasha could watch over the horse activities at the same time.

When she was old enough to crawl, the possibility of her getting too close to the horses became a problem. When Natasha was busy, it seemed natural that the Professor should appoint himself Tracey Helen's guardian.

By the time the little girl had her first birthday, the Professor had taught her to walk and from time to time he took her to meet some of the horses. As she got older, she was taught to ride; the Professor always seemed to have the time to supervise this. Natasha was very happy to have the Professor looking after her daughter; she could concentrate again on the affairs of the riding school.

Tracey was a regular visitor to the riding school, she felt a responsibility towards Natasha, and was a keen observer of all the activities there. She formed her own opinions, but very wisely kept them all to herself.

Natasha arranged to have Tracey Helen christened, before she was two years old, and Tracey was delighted to be named as her

Godmother. Natasha did not name either a father or a Godfather at this ceremony.

Tracey continued to keep her own council, and vigorously condemned any speculation that she heard on the parentage of her cherished Goddaughter.

CHAPTER TWENTYTWO.
EPILOGUE.

WHILE THE honeymooners were away, Mother Leong moved into her granny flat. She spent two days cleaning out the builders' debris and setting it up to her satisfaction. She then set about finding a job. Cleaning was what she knew best and she soon found a suitable position with the hotel where she and Tracey had been staying. Her new employers were impressed with her efficiency and dedication, it was obvious to them that if she chose to stay, and became fully conversant with the hotel, she would in a short time become their head cleaner. She liked the better pay and hours for cleaners in her new town, and enjoyed her work.

On their return from their honeymoon Tracey and Sam found that mother Leong, when she was not busy with her cleaning job, kept a very keen eye on them. Sam was forced to be a changed man, a man of mixed happiness. He found that he lived in some trepidation of his mother-in-law, whose word with her daughter was law indeed. Post hole boring eyes did not work with her, and many of those who had experienced those eyes quite enjoyed the sight of Sam quailing in front of the united Tracey and mum gaze of condemnation.

It was not long before Sam found that camp life with his fencers was at times more peaceful than that in town. Tracey was keen to help with his fencing, so elected to collect his stores and supplies and to bring them to his camp. With her experience of Toyotas in the Boeing rescue days, she soon qualified for her licence and then made regular trips to Sam's camp. There could be no more nonsense with little black cooks; Tracey's arrivals were at irregular times.

Tracey was good for business, the locals found she soon had a good grip of the details of contracting and so she kept Sam well supplied with work. Their finances were good.

Punch, Bruce, Chantelle and Judy carried on with their lives as they had before the crash. Chantelle soon found another "bloke" who suited her lifestyle; she stayed good friends with the Professor, who continued to keep his distance. Chantelle, ever practical, realised that their romance was over.

Kununurra became the centre of a series of "crash survivor weddings" in the next year, with Nugget and Adelaide, accompanied by "Mudlark" who was still in their care, Lance Park and Jane Burrows, Leslie Roberts and Harry Green exchanging their vows.

Then came the social event of the year, the joint weddings of Helen Anderson to Tony Khaw and Gwen Thomas to Hugh Wilkins. Now that was an event, international press, society magazine editors TV reporters all in a frenzy. The locals all enjoyed the pageant it presented and enjoyed the hospitality that Helen ensured was readily available.

The trauma of the crash and rescue was enough to weld a bond between the bush men, the crew of the Boeing, some of the survivors, all those who by their actions showed their compassion and concern for others. As they had learned to depend on each other in that time of stress and turmoil, so this bond remained with them. The "crash bushman" fellowship that resulted was very strong. It was a bond not understood by the media and society people., who found themselves outside of it. It was very real and treasured, maintained by the members over many years in the future, nurtured by reunions of the members whenever an excuse to revisit Kununurra arose.

Helen was for ever grateful to the bushmen who organised her rescue, and in particular to Sam and the Professor who stood up so strongly for her and her companions when the Corporation men were totally ignoring her at Brolga Springs. The Corporation jet was a familiar visitor to the Kununurra Airport, with such regular visits from Helen and Gwen.

The Professor was several times offered a job by Helen, but he politely and gratefully declined. He was, he said, quite happy with his lifestyle, no great hassles, working in his chosen field, when contracts surfaced or when the mood or opportunity faced him, with his friends around him; who needed regular hours and obligations?

The Professor, through Gwen, was given the task of monitoring the affairs of the bushmen, and to advise Helen if they thought she could help them in any difficulties that they met. This was done quietly when needed, in a manner if possible that was entirely anonymous. The knowledge to Helen that she was the "Fairy Godmother" to her bush friends was reward enough.

The End.

The End.

GLOSSARY.

4WD.	Any vehicle fitted with four wheel drive facility. (US "SUV")
Backpackers.	Young economy tourists-hitchhikers who stay at youth hostels.
Barramundi.	Prized game fish of North Australian Rivers.
BBC	Nickname for a constant talker-never off the air; hence BBC. Affectionate diminutive "BB." used in conversation.
Billy.	Billycan. Container with wire handle used in an open fire to boil water.
Bloke.	Guy. Chap.
Bogie.	Having a wash, a personal scrub up, usually at a water trough or in a creek.
Boabs.	Tropical boabab tree. It has a fat, tubby round fleshy trunk; often called bottle tree.
Bore.	Drill hole in ground to access water table to allow pumping.
Bundy.	Bundaburg Rum-or any rum.
Bullcatchers.	Cattlemen who catch wild, unmanageable bulls by chasing them with cut down 4WD vehicles, throwing them and pinning them down with the bull bar until they are tied up by the legs.
Bush.	To "bush" or to be "bushed." Sent away; disowned, no longer required.
Carton.	A carton of 2 dozen cans or small bottles of beer.

Chook.	Aussie name for chicken or hen.
Chookhouse.	Local nickname for a State Government building in Kununurra clad with corrugated iron like a "chook pen."
Creole.	Local pigeon. Part English, part Aboriginal language.
Dingo.	Wild Aust. native dog.
Donga.	Temporary makeshift shelter in Military jargon. Transportable building civilian slang.
Drum.	Steel oil barrel-40 imperial gallons-55 U.S.-200 litres.
Dry.	The season of winter in the Tropics-usually cold with minimal or no rain.
"Eyee", "eyee"	Creole for yes. Slurred rendition of " that's right."?
Grog.	Any alcoholic drink-especially beer.
Gulong.	Creole word for beer.
Grazier.	Australian for Rancher.
Hoochie.	Small personal makeshift shelter- 1-4 persons.
Leg Pullers.	Tellers of tall stories-not necessarily true.
Motor car.	Old bushman name for any motor vehicle or small truck. Used often in Creole.
Mob.	A group. A number of people or things-in large numbers "Biggest Mobs."
NT.	Northern Territory of Australia-Self Governing province.
Pastoralist.	Australian for Rancher.
Plods.	Policemen.
Pub.	Licensed hotel or bar.
Ringer.	Australian cowboy.
Spinifex.	Grass of the dessert and arid areas. Has long thin leaves with spikes on the end. A hostile plant.
Station.	Cattle station. Australian for ranch.

Stubbies.	Brief, black, elastic waist banded football type shorts. **OR** Small bottles of beer.
Swag.	Bush bed roll-canvas ground sheet-mattress-blanket/s- canvas top cover.
Thongs.	Rubber slip on sandal type footwear of Asian origin.
Tinned dog.	Any type of canned meat, particularly beef.
Tucker.	Food.
W.A.	The State of Western Australia. (Land area half the continent.)
Water Cooler.	Hand carried foam plastic insulated water container. (Chilly Bin in NZ.)
Wet, The	The summer season in the tropics, the season of much rain.
Whinger.	Person who constantly complains.
W.O.	Army rank Warrant Officer-Sergeant Major. Senior non commissioned officer.